STEPHANIE S. TOLAN

Welcome to the Ark

MORROW JUNIOR BOOKS

New York

*Special thanks are due to many people
without whose help the Ark could not have been launched:*

*Barry and Trudy for the Festivals
for their generous support
and for Debar, the magical place that became Laurel Mountain*

Jason for his technical assistance

Joanna for her poetry

*And especially to Meredith Charpentier
an editor with good courage, patience, an unerring eye,
and a caring heart.*

The three poems in this book—"Dream-Dust," "Tale of a Dreamer,"
and "Clouds chase across a woven field of rain"—
are copyright © 1996 by Joanna Michal Hoyt.
The poems were written by Ms. Hoyt between the ages of ten and
twelve and have been used with her permission.

Printed in the United States of America.

1   2   3   4   5   6   7   8   9   10

Library of Congress Cataloging-in-Publication Data
Tolan, Stephanie S.
Welcome to the Ark/Stephanie S. Tolan.
p. cm.
Summary: When four child prodigies transfer from a center for research and
rehabilitation to an experimental group home, they face another way of
connecting with their world.
ISBN 0-688-13724-5
[1. Gifted children—Fiction.   2. Family life—Fiction.]   I. Title.
PZ7.T5735We 1996   [Fic]—dc20   96-10163   CIP AC

This book is dedicated, with love and hope,
to the Festival kids:

Jake and Molly
Joanna and Zach
David and Joey
Ronnie and Ali
Russell, Erica, and Suzi
Bailey and Dylan
Jay and Carol
and
Shawn

Phenom Vanishes

Paris (AP)—Fifteen-year-old Miranda Ellenby, known to the world through her mother's best-selling book, *Phenom in the Family,* has disappeared from an academic conference on language and culture where she was to present a paper. She is the youngest person ever to be asked to participate in the elite international gathering. Ellenby was last seen by a doorman at her hotel yesterday when she left "for a walk" shortly after dawn. "We were to meet for breakfast," said Dr. Miriam Freidenberg, her companion and adviser at Harvard, where Ellenby is pursuing a doctorate in Romance languages and literature, "but she never appeared." French police have been joined in their investigation by Interpol. The girl's distraught father, Dr. Walter Ellenby, who has built a multimillion-dollar business aimed at teaching parents how to create geniuses, arrived in Paris this morning to join the search.

Miranda

In the late-afternoon sun, the girl in blue jeans and sneakers and a flowered warm-up jacket, her hair pushed up into a gold beret, was very still. Leaning over the bridge rail, she watched a *bateau-mouche* churn by beneath, stirring the dark water as it passed. She kept her head turned away from the figures moving on the busy sidewalk behind her. Among the stories of border conflicts and terrorist bombings, the morning papers in three languages had been full of her disappearance, her publicity photo from the conference brochure smiling out from the pages.

She sighed and reached into her jacket pocket to pull out an orange. It was the last remnant of the food she had bought yesterday—cheese, bread, fruit, pastries, sparkling water. The rest she had consumed in the shabby pension in Montmartre where she had spent the night. The concierge had asked no questions, accepting her accent, the way nearly everyone did, as Parisian, with a shadow of something that hinted, perhaps, of a country childhood.

She had not meant to run away. She had meant only to take a walk, as she had told the grandfatherly doorman who fussed about the dangers of the city and the chill of the misty morning air. But when it was time to go back she had found she couldn't. Something drew her on, farther and farther from the hotel, finally to have breakfast alone at a sidewalk café, watching people as the city woke up and went about its business. And then on again, first along the Seine, then into side streets, watching the people. Always watching the people. The woman pushing a baby carriage, the lovers leaning against a tree in a tiny park, their arms twined around each other. The old men on a bench, arguing in a dialect she could barely understand, one gesturing with his cigar, the other with a folded newspaper.

She had a sense that she was looking for something, something all those other people seemed to have. She didn't even know for certain what it was, only that in spite of speaking their language, the thing that should have made her one of them, she didn't have it. Had never had it.

Now she began peeling the orange, dropping the first bit of peel into the river below and watching the spot of color bob sideways in the fading wake, dipping and turning as it moved toward the line of foam and debris along the muddy bank beneath the bridge. The rest of the peel she put into her pocket. As she separated the segments, she thought about last night, the first night of her life when no one, not Mother or Daddy, not Miriam, not Dr. James, had been with her, or even known where she was. The first night of her life she had ever been truly alone.

She had sat by the window of the little room with the stained ceiling, staring out over the rooftops of Paris, silvered by moonlight. By morning she had made a decision. She would go back, of course. About that she had no choice. She would not explain her leaving—how could she when she didn't fully understand it herself? She would greet their questions with silence and let them invent their own stories. This evening she would present her paper on schedule. And when the conference ended she would fly home with Miriam.

But she would not continue the life her mother and father had planned for her.

When Miranda had finished the orange, her hands and mouth sticky with the juice, she turned toward the street and began to walk back to the hotel, keeping her head down, her eyes on her feet. As she walked, unnoticed among the hurrying people, even by the soldiers patrolling with their guns slung over their backs, she thought about what she had understood in the long, drifting quiet of the moonlit night. She had started learning languages all those years ago in a desperate search for her native tongue. She had never found it. She suspected now she never would.

3

BENEATH A BUSH IN THE corner of a playground shadowed by two towering apartment buildings a small boy in tattered blue jeans and a too-small jacket sat, writing with one dark brown finger in the dirt. T-O-N-D-I-S-H-I. He spelled it out and drew a line around it, the name of the world he had built in his mind and filled with animals and people of his own design.

Early this morning the growling sound had begun in his head and he had hurried outside, to this refuge he had swept clean of broken glass and stones. All summer when the growl began—the growl that meant the man would be yelling soon, throwing things, looking for a reason to hit or punch or kick—he had done his best to get outside, to hide here with the smell of dirt and green leaves and tell himself stories of Tondishi, a world of open skies and mountains and meadows like the ones he remembered from before they came to the city.

Sometimes he made it out, sometimes he didn't. Soon, he knew, the leaves would fall and this safe place would be gone. Even if he could get out of the apartment in time, he would have to find somewhere else to hide. Now he wrote S-A-M-S-O-N slowly in the dirt, the Bible name he had borrowed for the wild-living, cave-dwelling Tondishi hero he liked best, a tall, strong, dark man who had no need to hide, whose story he had been telling himself this morning.

The growl had grown, as it so often did now, into a roar, so loud in his head that he couldn't think. He had lost his hold on the story. The roar meant that the man inside was yelling now, smashing things against the walls. He hoped his mother had left, but he couldn't be sure. He'd tried to warn her in the old way, thinking the warning at her as hard as he could, but she hadn't understood. She hardly ever understood anymore. He struggled to find the sense of her through the roaring in his head. It was there, a fragile thread of warmth that, before the man came into their lives, had glowed bright and strong. His mother was still inside, frightened, making herself as quiet and as small as she could.

Suddenly there was a flash, so vivid it seemed to blind him, even though it was inside his head, had nothing more to do with his eyes than the roar had to do with his ears. He blinked. Darkness. And silence, so sudden, so complete that it nearly knocked him over. Frantically, he searched for the thread of warmth, knowing the truth even as he searched. It was gone. Gone. There was nothing but cold, darkness, silence.

Then the roar exploded like a bottle against a wall. He wrapped both arms around his head, as if to shut it out. Beneath the roar the darkness was as empty as it had been the night Mama Effie died.

Mama, too, was gone. He was alone. Tears filled his eyes and spilled over.

For a long, long time Elijah did not move. Then he raised his head, rubbed out the letters in the dirt, wiped his nose on his jacket sleeve, and filled his mind with a white fog that blotted out thoughts and memories and, when they came, the sound of the sirens.

THE BOY SAT ON THE rough wooden platform he had built long ago in the fork of an ancient tree, his legs crossed, calves resting against heavy hiking boots. His camouflage jacket was buttoned tightly and his breath made little puffs of mist in the air. A Day-Glo orange cap lay beside him. His head, pale scalp showing through his black crew cut, was exposed like a penance to the cold. In his hands he held a rifle with a hunting scope. Fifteen feet from the tree, in the center of the sloped, rock-strewn clearing, a mound of alfalfa stood out against the tan clutter of fallen leaves. No deer had scented it, for which he gave a silent thanks. It had been a long time since he had gotten away with missing his shot. But the sun was just rising above the mountains. There were hours to go yet.

From time to time a hollow popping sound echoed up and down the slopes. He gave no sign of hearing, having learned to shut the sound out. But now he heard rustling among the trees on the far side of the clearing. A person, he thought. More than one. He tensed, his hands tightening on his gun. Game wardens seldom ventured far from the roads, but anytime, anywhere in the vast stretch of Adirondack wilderness, militia members could appear. The Free Mountain Militia—armed and unpredictable. A distant gunshot sounded, and he relaxed. Unpredictable yes, stupid certainly, but not stupid enough to risk war games during hunting season.

Three figures emerged from the heavy cover of the pines, across the clearing to his right. Each was dressed as the boy was dressed, except that their hats were firmly in place, bright earflaps down. Each carried a gun, barrel pointed at the ground. His father and older brothers. They moved upward steadily, watching their footing on the frozen ground.

In a smooth, practiced move, the boy lifted his rifle and looked into the scope, moving so that first one and then another head was centered in the crosshairs. A tremor ran up his spine and time seemed to slow. It would be so easy. One finger. Not much more effort than fingering a flute. Wasn't this what they were all out here for? The manly art of taking life? It would be a hunting accident. They happened all the time.

Except that it could be only one of them. There were no accidents that took down three.

Doug moved the barrel so that his father's head was the target, centered it carefully. Then, with a long, shuddering breath, he set the gun, its safety still on, next to the hat beside him. The head tilted back and the dark eyes met his across the steadily shrinking distance.

"John got a five-point buck," John McAllister called, the pride in his echoing voice as ordinary as breathing. "Let's get it home."

January 26, 2000 _____
TARYN

SNOW SWIRLED AGAINST THE WINDOWS of the Laurel Mountain Center for Research and Rehabilitation, so that the distant mountains, the lake, even the nearest trees were blotted out in the white turbulence. The wind howled around the corners of the building.

In the arts and activities room a little boy, huddled under a table, began to beat his head against the table leg and moan with the wind. Other voices joined him, some children stamping feet, others pounding on the tables, until the cacophony overrode the sound from outside. The art therapist and her assistant hurried from child to child, murmuring, patting, calming.

Next to the window a small hand was pressed against the cold glass. A child with hair that fell in a fine black sheet down her narrow back sat still and silent, peering out into the storm. She frowned in concentration and raised the other hand to press it, too, against the glass. The snow whispered against the window, a tiny sound she could just pick out beneath the background din. The snow had stories to tell, stories of silent mountains, sleeping trees, the frozen surface of the lake and the life suspended far beneath. Stories of cold and darkness and danger.

She leaned to touch her forehead to the window, shivering in the draft. And felt something else, something far beyond the storm, beyond the mountains. It was not a voice, not a sound or even a vision. The child closed her eyes to focus. It was no use. As she tried to bring it in it skidded sideways, out of reach. A change was coming, she thought, an important change. But she couldn't make it clearer than that. She opened her eyes again, listening to the whispers of the snow. The winter stories were stories of waiting. She could wait. It was the most important thing she had learned here.

Gathering

Laurel Mountain Center for Research and Rehabilitation

PATIENT NUMBER	LAST NAME FIRST NAME M.I.	DATE ADMITTED	
5042	Ellenby, Miranda K.	6/5/00	

LEGAL STATUS AT ADMISSION	AGE	SEX	RACE
Involuntary	16y, 3m	F	W

HOME ADDRESS	EDUCATIONAL STATUS AT ADMISSION	CITY & STATE OF BIRTH
50 Green Meadow Dr. Waltham, MA 02154	B.A. + grad. work	Waltham, MA

FATHER'S NAME	ADDRESS PHONE	OCCUPATION
Walter J. Ellenby	50 Green Meadow Dr. Waltham, MA 02154 617-555-4307	Prof.—Harvard Pres.—Phenom, Ltd.

MOTHER'S MAIDEN NAME	ADDRESS PHONE	OCCUPATION
Elizabeth Stern	(see above)	Writer Dir.—Phenom, Ltd.

PARENTS' MARITAL STATUS	PERSON TO NOTIFY IN EMERGENCY PHONE	RELATIONSHIP
M	Walter or Elizabeth Ellenby 617-555-4307	Parents

ESTABLISHED DIAGNOSIS	DIAGNOSTIC IMPRESSION AT ADMISSION
Referring phys. suggests possible borderline personality	No diagnosis possible.

ADDITIONAL NOTES REGARDING ADMISSION INTERVIEW

Subject totally uncooperative. Spoke only to insist on her "Miranda rights."

PREVIOUS HOSPITALIZATION	INSTITUTION	DATES: FROM TO	
None			

ADMITTING PHYSICIAN	SIGNATURE	DATE
Harlan Turnbull	*Harlan Turnbull*	6/5/00

Journal—Miranda Ellenby
June 6, 2000—10:30 P.M.

It was the interview I did with KIDS TODAY *magazine—where I said I was an alien—that pushed them over the edge. From the moment they read it, they started looking at me funny. Really funny. Not like the way they looked at me when I shaved my head. This was out of the sides of their eyes, and there was desperation in it. Up till then, they'd figured I was just doing an adolescent number on them. After the interview they put it all together, everything I'd done since Paris, and came to the conclusion that I was having a mental meltdown. Maybe they're right. For the smartest kid in the world, it was a pretty stupid mistake.*

*It never occurred to me that anyone would think I was really crazy. Or that looking crazy in public would demolish (*PTURFLUKT!*) the Ellenby empire. If Mother and Daddy made me what I was before, now it would look to all the world as if they'd made me nuts, too. Who would sign up for another workshop? Who would buy another book?*

Mother must have worked fast to get them that appearance on Delia Shevin's CNN *talk show for the very day the magazine would hit the stands. Craziness was never mentioned, of course. Teen rebellion was their story. "Adolescence is a difficult period for any child, doubly so for a prodigy, and Miranda needs some time away from the public spotlight." Right. So very quietly, with lots of security, they dumped me here.*

Once they decided I was crazy nothing I said would change their minds. Crazy people can't plan their lives, of course—

everybody knows that. Besides, kids—no matter how smart they are—have no power in the world. None.

Did I believe the alien story when I told the woman who was doing the interview? Do I now? It isn't such a bad explanation, given how different I am from them—from everybody. I could have been traded for Baby Ellenby by the aliens I really belonged to right there in the hospital before anybody knew the real one well enough to notice the difference. Left on earth by aliens, waiting for them to come back and take me home.

When I was little I used to stand and stare up at the stars and wonder which one of them held the solar system that was my real home. I toyed with the idea that Mother and Daddy were in on the switch—a way to get a baby and fortune and fame at the same time. Of course, if they'd been in on it, they wouldn't have sent me here. Besides, I think they really believe they made me what I am. After all, they got me a psychologist and all those tutors and let me go to college when I was nine. Hardly standard parenting practice. Nobody seems to notice that no matter how many parents take the Ellenby workshops, their kids just don't manage to turn out like me. Phenom, Ltd. is right. The phenomenon is limited to me.

So here I am at the Laurel Mountain Center for Research and Rehabilitation (a private nuthouse), with nobody to talk to except shrinks and loonies. Writing my journal on the computer the shrinks agreed to install in my private room (got to give Mother and Daddy that—they're sparing no expense), writing in Muktuluk so I don't have to worry about any tricks they might have built into the system to spy on me.

It's like when I was little and wrote my diary in Muktuluk so Mother and Daddy's snooping wouldn't do them any good. I'd figured out that there were two uses for language—to connect people who speak it and to keep out people who don't. I used to talk in Muktuluk, too. Nobody understood it was a whole language, grammar, syntax, and all. They thought I was just playing.

Of course, I had to quit speaking it and erase all my computer discs when I was ten and Mother's book came out. The army of psychologists and linguistics people that descended on me after the book would have had a field day if they'd found it. They were freaked enough that I knew so many real languages. It would have been even worse if they'd known I made one up on my own when I was three.

I never stopped thinking in Muktuluk, though, and growing it. So there aren't many ideas I can't express this way—and some I can't manage properly in any other language. No need to hide Muktuluk now—what can happen to me that's worse than being committed?

Judging from the people I've met so far—especially Turnbull, the head shrink—I can safely assume nobody here is going to be able to come up with a translation, even if they have some way of finding this. The big problem here, like everywhere else, won't be whether anybody's sharp enough to figure me out, but whether I can suffer the fools gladly. Or suffer them at all.

Hey, up there on Home Planet, time to beam me up! Joke's over. Experiment's done. I want to come home now. Do you hear me?

TRANSCRIPT, INITIAL THERAPY SESSION
PATIENT: Miranda Ellenby
PRIMARY THERAPIST: Harlan Turnbull, M.D., Ph.D.

TURNBULL: So. Here we are again. How was breakfast?

MIRANDA: Please convey my compliments to the chef. Exquisite Cheerios. Positively exquisite.

TURNBULL: Would you mind turning your chair around? [scraping sound] Actually, I suppose I meant halfway around. One hundred eighty degrees, not three sixty. I find it disconcerting to speak to someone's back.

MIRANDA: It's not a bad back. My mother thinks my hair's my best feature. You see lots more of it this way.

TURNBULL: Miranda.

MIRANDA: All right. [scraping sound] How's this?

TURNBULL: Thank you. I hope you're going to be a little more cooperative today.

MIRANDA: I'll consider it.

TURNBULL: Good. [sound of paper shuffling] All right, then. According to an interview you did for *Kids Today*—

MIRANDA: No.

TURNBULL: I beg your pardon?

MIRANDA: I said, "No." No, I do not actually believe I'm an alien. That's what you were starting to ask me, wasn't it?

TURNBULL: Well, yes...

MIRANDA: Frankly, I'm surprised you jumped to that question first thing. I would have thought you'd work up to it slowly. I mean, it's the critical question, isn't it?

TURNBULL: [clears throat] Well...

MIRANDA: In any case, you can scratch "delusions."

TURNBULL: Scratch—?

MIRANDA: Off your list of symptoms. I do not have delusions of being an alien. No matter how much it would explain.

TURNBULL: [pause] Suppose you let me actually finish a question before you provide the answer.

MIRANDA: I was just trying to be a little more cooperative today.

TURNBULL: Try not to overdo it.

MIRANDA: Okay. [long pause, sound of paper shuffling] Of course, you do have to ask a question if I'm going to let you finish it before I answer.

TURNBULL: I would prefer it if you would let me conduct the interview.

MIRANDA: I read somewhere that psychiatrists tend to have controlling personalities. Sorry if I stepped on your toes.

TURNBULL: You did not—

MIRANDA: Metaphorically speaking, of course. Your professional toes. Don't you think it's interesting that so many metaphors about pushiness involve feet in some way? I stepped over the line, stepped into your territory, stepped out of bounds. Do you suppose it indicates some sort of fetish in our culture? Maybe it's just *Homo sapiens*'s pride in walking upright.

TURNBULL: Perhaps we should begin again.

MIRANDA: Right. See if we can get off on the right foot. I'll do my best to toe the line.

TURNBULL: When did you first notice that you were different from other children?

MIRANDA: [pause] Different? Are you telling me I'm *different*?

TURNBULL: Please answer the question, Miranda.

MIRANDA: [response unintelligible]

TURNBULL: In English, please.

MIRANDA: Sorry. Is that a rule?

TURNBULL: I'm aware that you speak many languages. I speak English. If you'd like a rule about it, we can make a rule. From now on, I'd like you to answer my questions in English.

MIRANDA: It's a shame, really. Not the rule—speaking only one language. I assume you read the papers—the world's blowing itself apart because people don't understand each other and people, Americans especially, actually think it's sane to speak nothing but their own language. Ah well, if we're going to blow up, we're going to blow up. *C'est la vie.* Oh. Sorry. That's life. Or death, really, given the context.

TURNBULL: How about answering my question.

MIRANDA: Can you repeat it? I'm afraid I've forgotten what it was.

TURNBULL: When did you first notice that you were different from other children?

MIRANDA: That's a hard question to answer in any language.

Can we start with something a little easier?

TURNBULL: [with a deep sigh] Fine. How about we start with the easiest questions of all. First question: What is your name?

MIRANDA: Miranda Karen Ellenby.

TURNBULL: Second question: How old are you?

MIRANDA: I thought you were starting with the easiest ones. That's as hard as the other one. Harder even.

TURNBULL: You find it hard to tell me how old you are?

MIRANDA: Of course.

TURNBULL: Make a stab at it.

MIRANDA: Sixteen slash thirty-five.

TURNBULL: [pause] Excuse me?

MIRANDA: Don't tell me my scores aren't in my file.

TURNBULL: Scores?

MIRANDA: IQ scores. I've taken enough tests. The only one I didn't ceiling out on gave me an IQ of two twenty-two. Intelligence quotient—mental age divided by chronological age times one hundred. The math's simple enough. Two twenty-two times sixteen divided by one hundred—voila!—thirty-five point five. My mental age. It's a joke, of course. Mental age has no meaning at all after childhood. There are plenty of forty-year-old men still mentally stuck in their teens.

TURNBULL: You care quite a lot about that IQ score, don't you?

MIRANDA: [a short laugh] Maybe less than anybody.

18

Journal—Miranda Ellenby
June 7, 2000—11:30 P.M.

Got stuck staring into the mirror tonight. Standing there at the sink with my wet toothbrush in my hand, and that girl named Tookie in her bra and pants jabbering away at the sink next to me on one side and Florence, the girl with the red hair that looks like she cut it herself with manicure scissors, at the sink on the other, I tried to see if I looked different. Crazy. But everything was the same. Same eyes, same face, same hair.

Mother used to say I was lucky to have the hair I have—her wave and Daddy's color, shiny brown with glints of red, and lots of it. That's one of the reasons I shaved it all off, to get rid of her wave and his color. To stay bald, though, I'd have had to shave it every day, the way men shave their faces. An act of rebellion loses something if you have to repeat it daily like brushing your teeth.

I knew the reflection I was looking at all too well. Pale skin, long ears, long face, long body, long fingers, long legs. Being so tall always made it seem as if my body was trying to catch up to my mind, which it couldn't quite manage. It was useful, though. A thirteen-year-old in graduate school can't fit in, no matter what, but at least if she's tall enough, she doesn't look like somebody who got lost on her way to a Girl Scout meeting.

Back when I was fourteen and had that crush on Alex Trautman, the underage Ph.D. candidate in Russian literature, I was desperate to be shorter and to have a sexier figure. Boobs at least. It wouldn't have helped. Underage or not, he was still

19

twenty-two and had his sights set on that Russian exchange student—Ludmila. How could I have a boyfriend, anyway? I've never found a guy, including Alex Trautman, that I didn't scare half to death.

The accommodations aren't half bad, I'll give them that. Indoor pool, tennis courts, computer lab. Like a cross between a school and a resort, except for the iron fence around the grounds. And the metal ankle bracelets with a little chip that sets off an alarm if we get too near the fence or other boundaries—like the line of white stones that separates the lawn from the beach.

This afternoon I slathered myself with insect repellent to ward off the blackflies and went out to soak up the scenery (which is spectacular) and, just incidentally, try to figure out if escape from this place is possible. I found a bench down near the boathouse (one assumes they have boats, but what's the point if we can't go near the lake?) and spent most of the afternoon there. The answer about escape is maybe, but it would take some doing. This place is deep in the wilderness, so even if I got past the alarm and the fence, I could get lost trying to bushwhack my way back to civilization. They'd find my bones a hundred years from now. Assuming human beings make it that long.

LAUREL MOUNTAIN CENTER FOR RESEARCH AND REHABILITATION

PATIENT NUMBER	LAST NAME FIRST NAME M.I.	DATE ADMITTED	
5023	Raymond, Elijah G.	10/20/99	

LEGAL STATUS AT ADMISSION	AGE	SEX	RACE
Involuntary	8y, 2m	M	B

HOME ADDRESS	EDUCATIONAL STATUS AT ADMISSION	CITY & STATE OF BIRTH
c/o Children's Protective Services, Newark, NJ	(unknown)	Franklinton, NC

FATHER'S NAME	ADDRESS PHONE	OCCUPATION
(unknown)	(N/A)	(unknown)

MOTHER'S MAIDEN NAME	ADDRESS PHONE	OCCUPATION
Felicia Raymond	(deceased)	(N/A)

PARENTS' MARITAL STATUS	PERSON TO NOTIFY IN EMERGENCY PHONE	RELATIONSHIP
(N/A)	Children's Protective Services 201-555-7832	(N/A)

ESTABLISHED DIAGNOSIS	DIAGNOSTIC IMPRESSION AT ADMISSION
(N/A)	Infantile autism—classic symptoms. No eye contact, no speech, rocking motion, reacts negatively to being touched.

ADDITIONAL NOTES REGARDING ADMISSION INTERVIEW

Little information available on this child. Mother died in domestic dispute, 10/7/99. No relation in residence. Mother's companion, in police custody, claimed never to have heard the boy speak. Abuse suspected but not proved. CPS workers interviewed neighbors for further information, with little result. One elderly neighbor claimed child spoke until great-grandmother (who thought him extremely bright) died in 1997. No corroboration of this information available. Enrolled in school briefly, 9/96; quit attending 10/96—no follow-up. Foster care 10/8/99-10/20/99.
Communication with child impossible at this time.

PREVIOUS HOSPITALIZATION	INSTITUTION	DATES: FROM TO	
(N/A)			

ADMITTING PHYSICIAN	SIGNATURE	DATE
John Devereux	*John Devereux*	10/20/99

AT THE TABLE IN THE conference room, three people sat with identical stacks of manila folders in front of them, waiting for the 8:30 planning meeting to begin. John Devereux, child psychiatrist, crunched pretzels from a cellophane bag and washed them down with diet Coke. Abigail Periodes, clinical psychologist, sipped a cup of herbal tea, and Noah Periodes, clinical psychologist and Abigail's husband, leaned his chair back at a dangerous angle and held himself there with his knees under the table's edge. In his large hands he held a white coffee mug with the words DON'T PANIC on both sides. "What's your bet?" he asked Devereux.

Devereux checked his watch. "It was six minutes last time. I'll go eight."

"Twelve," Abigail said. "The more important he feels, the longer he makes us wait. With Miranda Ellenby here, he's bound to be in emperor mode."

"Fifteen," Noah said.

"I'll take side bets on how many days before he suggests putting her on meds," Devereux said. "If she lives up to her press, she'll have him running in circles."

When Harlan Turnbull, director of the Laurel Mountain Center, came into the room, his white coat open over a gray pinstriped suit, his arms full of folders, the others glanced at the clock over the door. 8:43. *I win,* Abigail mouthed.

Turnbull dropped his files at the head of the table and pulled out his leather chair. "I'm sure you understand that Miranda Ellenby's presence at Laurel Mountain is something of a coup." He seated himself with the gravity of a Supreme Court judge, took

22

a handkerchief out of his breast pocket, and wiped his pale pink forehead. "I went to school with a friend of her father's. The Ellenbys need to be assured that she's getting the best possible care, of course, so I'll be her primary." He folded his handkerchief and replaced it carefully.

Noah and Abigail exchanged glances. Noah shook his head ever so slightly. Neither of them spoke.

"So...what's your diagnosis?" Devereux asked.

Turnbull cleared his throat. "I wouldn't care to jump to any conclusions at this early date."

As Turnbull straightened the files in front of him Devereux winked at the others, hiding a grin behind his Coke can.

"Now. Let's get started. I'd like to begin with Elijah Raymond."

Abigail inhaled the steam rising from her tea and touched Noah's sandaled foot with her own. Noah nodded. Elijah Raymond's file was already on top of both their stacks. Devereux shuffled folders to find it.

Turnbull, his pale eyebrows knit in a thoughtful frown, turned to Devereux. "You've been his primary, John. Let's put aside a discussion of what has been going on in the last week and broaden our scope. What's your overall estimation of the effects of our efforts with this patient thus far?"

Devereux brushed salt from his flowered tie and shook his head. "Can't say there's been much change. Tippy has worked with him extensively in the pool. When he's in the water, he seems less traumatized by human touch. But as soon as he's out, we're back to square one. Gloria's had no luck with art. He resists her every effort. Janet thought she was getting his attention with some computer graphics and simple words back in November, but that faded quickly. She suspected the change was connected to Timmy Lasko's being scheduled into the lab during the same period—"

"Timmy the Terror," Abigail said. "I'd buy that. I thought you had upped his medication again, Harlan."

"His reactions have not been normal," Turnbull said stiffly. "I'm considering making another change."

"At any rate," Devereux continued, "Timmy assaulted several children and smashed a monitor screen before he was permanently barred from the computer lab. Janet tried to work with Elijah alone after that, but the glimmer she'd seen had disappeared. From what I know of this child, that glimmer might have been wishful thinking on Janet's part in the first place. I've seen Elijah three times a week since October, and I haven't been able to make any real contact." Devereux drained his Coke can. "Autism as profound as this is tough."

"So what you're saying, John, is that in the eight months Elijah Raymond has been with us we have struck out completely."

Devereux nodded sadly. "Things seem best for him when we leave him in his corner to rock."

"This seems, then, a reasonable time to try drug therapy."

Noah let his chair down with a bang.

"Harlan," Devereux said, "you know there's no research showing drugs to be effective in treating infantile autism!"

"I intend to use a combination that has never been tried. Since psychological factors have been pretty well ruled out in autism, I'm convinced we're looking at a problem of brain chemistry."

"Surprise, surprise," Noah muttered into his coffee mug.

24

"Not necessarily," Devereux said. "It could be a congenital defect in brain structure. Or brain organization."

Turnbull shook his head. "To me, the delay in onset very clearly suggests brain chemistry…"

"It's a moot point in this case," Abigail interrupted. "With Elijah, we're not dealing with autism at all."

"What? Of course we are." Turnbull's pink face grew pinker, his thin lips thinner. "That's been the diagnosis since he was admitted."

Devereux nodded. "He's a classic case, Abigail. Extreme withdrawal, repetitive motions, language deficit, preference for objects over people, refusal to make eye contact, intense response to sensory input—it's a near-textbook list of symptoms. I've seen him spinning that marble he carries with him for literally hours at a time. And he goes berserk when he's touched."

Abigail sipped her tea before speaking. "Did you know he reads?"

Turnbull's eyebrows arced toward his thinning hairline. "Reads? Elijah Raymond? He can't even speak."

"*Doesn't* speak," Noah said. "Don't you remember the social workers' report? A neighbor told them he spoke perfectly well until his great-grandmother died a couple of years ago."

Devereux riffled through papers in the file in front of him. "I distinctly remember that the stepfather said he'd never heard a single word out of him."

"That man had been in Elijah's life less than a year. The neighbor had lived in the building since Elijah's family moved there from the mountains of North Carolina. She said the great-grandmother thought Elijah was some kind of genius."

"Hardly reliable information on which to base a diagnosis," Turnbull said.

"Infantile autism shows itself before age three. Elijah seems not to have shut down until age six." Abigail held up a typed page. "If we piece together what the social workers gathered, we can't rule out psychological factors in this case. Pathological withdrawal caused by trauma."

"What makes you think the boy can read?" Devereux asked.

"I've seen him."

"What we believe is apt to be what we see," Noah said, and waved his mug, so that he dripped coffee on his jeans. "We were all looking through lenses that said autism. Abigail had the good sense to take them off."

"I noticed him pressing his forehead against the glass door of the library," Abigail explained, "for all the world like a kid staring into a candy shop. He can hardly pass the place without doing it."

"So," Noah said, "she gathered a bunch of books—"

"From picture books to novels," Abigail put in.

"And put them in his corner of the living room. She told everybody to leave them there but watch to see whether he noticed them."

"Nothing happened for a couple of days," Abigail said. "And then one of the aides saw him running his hand over the books. Then nothing for a day. Then I found him rocking as usual, in his usual place, with one of the books open in his lap. He was shielding it, so I had to make an effort to see he had it. I sat on the floor myself, against the wall, where I could see very clearly. He was

26

concentrating so hard I'm sure he didn't even know I was there. That vacant look had vanished, and his attention was more like a laser beam. Judging from the rate he was turning the pages, he not only reads, he reads very, very fast. The book, gentlemen, was *Treasure Island.*"

"He could have been merely turning the pages." The fingers of Turnbull's right hand drummed the table as he spoke.

"I am quite certain he was reading, Harlan."

"So—perhaps he's a savant."

Devereux turned to Abigail. "There *are* autistic savants who read fluently but have no understanding of content. Could that be what he was doing?"

"I watched his face as he read. And I can tell you, he understood."

Devereux extracted the last pretzel and crushed the bag into a ball. "For eight months I've seen nothing but blankness behind those eyes. I hope you don't mind if I don't throw away my diagnosis on the spot."

"The technicality of the diagnosis doesn't really matter," Noah said. "The home is finished and we're all moved in. It's time to begin the Global Family Group Home project. Abigail and I have decided that Elijah Raymond should be the first member of our family group."

Turnbull stopped drumming the table. "No."

"I beg your pardon?"

"I said no, Noah. I don't think that's an appropriate placement. You've made it very clear that the point of your experiment is connection. Intense human connection within the therapeutic family and electronically around the world. Elijah Raymond is unable to connect at all! Besides, as I've said, I have other plans—"

"Have you forgotten the board's decision, Harlan?" Abigail was smiling, but her soft voice had an edge to it. "We have to be free to choose any child in the center. Otherwise, the experiment can't possibly work."

Noah set Elijah Raymond's file to the left of his stack of folders and looked steadily at Turnbull. "This one isn't your call. According to the board, it's ours. And we've chosen Elijah."

Harlan—
In case
you've misplaced
your copy
—Noah

August 5, 1999

Noah and Abigail Periodes
1458 Spruce Hill Rd.
Laurel Ridge, NY 12929

Dear Drs. Periodes,

It is with great pleasure that I write to inform you that the board has given the final go-ahead for your Global Family Group Home Project (GFGHP). Full funding has been authorized by the foundation, and we hope to break ground for the home itself in a matter of weeks. If we can get it under roof before winter so that the interior work can be done during the cold weather, it ought to be ready for occupancy by next summer.

As you know, there has been some concern on the part of a few board members over the high cost of the communication technology. However, at the last board meeting your eloquent defense of the focus on connections for the patients, not just within the family but around the world, reminded us all that this is what distinguishes your project from other group homes and could make Laurel Mountain the focus of international attention. Instead of the isolation so many disturbed children face during treatment, your "family" members will have the opportunity to establish safe, well-monitored electronic social interactions that should smooth their eventual return to the outside world.

Dr. Turnbull has reiterated his belief that as director he should have the final word on placement. However, the board remains convinced that the success of this therapeutic family depends on careful selection of the members. As the creators of the project, the two of you would seem to be best qualified to make that selection. The project has been approved exactly *as your proposal defined it.*

You might be interested to know that the vote was unanimous. We are all eager to see the Global Family Group Home Project in operation as soon as possible.

Sincerely,

Harold Deitz

Harold Deitz, President of the Board
cc: Harlan Turnbull, M.D., Ph.D.

Journal—Miranda Ellenby
June 9, 2000—6:45 A.M.

Half an hour ago I woke up from a dream, and I can't get back to sleep. It wasn't like a regular dream, all choppy and strange. It was more like a story. And I remember every bit of it, down to the tiniest detail.

When it began, I was riding a horse. It was a blue-black horse, sleek and shiny, with a long mane and a tail that almost dragged on the ground. The saddle was all silver and red tassels, with a bridle to match.

I was holding the reins, but not really directing the horse. He was just cantering along through a field of grass. Not a field exactly, because there weren't any fences or borders. Just tall grass as far as I could see, right to the horizon. An ocean of grass. The wind moved it in waves, in patterns. The light was sort of gray-blue, like dawn. And it was chilly. I could feel goose bumps on my arms. But it wasn't only the cold that gave me goose bumps. I was scared. I could feel somebody coming behind me. Not visible, yet, but coming, following me. Somebody or something.

We came to a river, with a steep sandy bank down to it. The river was shallow and fast-moving, with stones and boulders here and there where the water foamed and splashed. We galloped through it with spray flying up on either side, and then we were up the opposite bank and into the grass again. On the far horizon I could just see the blue shapes of mountains, but they were so far and so faint, they might have been banks of clouds instead of mountains. Clouds or smoke.

30

Ahead, about halfway to the horizon, there was a cottage. It was low and made of stone, with a thatched roof. Smoke was coming out of its chimney. And standing on the peak of the roof next to the chimney was a black bird with a heavy black beak. The horse was heading straight for the cottage, and when we got close, he slowed and came to a stop.

I don't remember dismounting; just suddenly I was standing at the door. It was one of those split doors, where the top can open separately from the bottom. The top was open now. Inside I could see a small dark room with a fire burning in a fireplace. There were two chairs near it, with their backs to me. I opened the bottom half of the door and went in.

One of the two chairs was a rocking chair, and an old woman sat there, knitting. The other was more like an easy chair, and there was an old man in it, carving something with a small knife. They both looked up, and though they didn't say anything, I could tell they'd been expecting me. The woman put down her needles and held out what she had been knitting. At first I thought it was a scarf, but then it became a sweater, the off-white of an Irish fisherman's sweater. It was a cardigan, though, and up and down the button and buttonhole edges flowers were embroidered in colors that were soft and vivid at the same time. Pinks and yellows and blues and greens.

"Put it on," the woman said, and I did. It fit. I'd expected it to be scratchy, but it was so soft and light I hardly knew I had it on. "Warm enough," she said, and I nodded, but it wasn't a question. "Warm enough," she repeated.

Then the old man pushed himself up from his chair. I saw what he'd been working on. It was a wooden whistle. It had

31

several fingering holes and was covered with intricately carved designs—of flowers and birds and trees and animals, all woven together, so you couldn't tell quite where one image began and another ended. I thought he was going to give it to me, so I held out my hand. But he didn't. He pointed with it toward the fire.

There was a cat curled on a hearth rug. It was snowy white, its eyes a brilliant almost glowing green. It stared at me so hard that I blinked, and when I looked again, it was a gray-and-black-striped tabby. A very ordinary-looking cat. Only the eyes were the same. "To keep her safe," the old man explained, as if he'd read my thoughts. "White cats are too easy to see. Too easy to remember. But she'll be white again when she needs to be." This didn't seem at all strange to me. "She'll go with you."

I nodded as the cat came over and rubbed against my legs. I picked her up and held her against my cheek, and her whole body vibrated with purring.

The old man hobbled toward the door and held it open. "Go now. The time is coming and you have much to do. Be careful."

"Good-bye," I said to the old woman, who had gone back to her knitting. Already she seemed to have another garment on her needles, well begun. She smiled, but nodded without speaking. "Thank you," I said.

As I carried the cat through the door, the old man frowned. "Much depends on you," he said, and I sensed he was speaking to the cat as well as to me.

The horse was stamping with impatience when I reached him. I put the cat, which was back to being white now, onto the saddle. Then I mounted, and the cat was somehow curled *against me as the horse began to move toward the distant mountains. I turned to look back at the cottage, but it was gone. Shivering, I looked up and saw the bird overhead, circling high above us against the brightening sky. Then the horse began to put on speed and we were running again, with very little feeling of movement except the wind in my hair. The white cat purred steadily in my lap as we went. The bird, barely moving its wings, kept pace with us as the sun rose. Behind me I heard the rumble of thunder. Or heavy guns.*

And then I was awake. Beige walls, gray-green nubby bedspread, window with diamond panes to disguise the fact of bars, and the mountain going pink in the sunrise, a little cap of clouds hovering around its peak.

The dream came with me when I woke up. It didn't disappear or even start to fade. It was just there the way a book is still there in your head when you finish reading it. And so was the sense of distant but growing threat.

June 9, 2000_____

MIRANDA HAD TOLD THE RECREATION therapist she'd nicknamed Polly Perky that she didn't play tennis. The prospect of seeing the sun glint off the ever-so-white teeth of that perpetual smile through a whole tennis match was more than she could bear.

Instead, she went to the bench by the boathouse, the spot she had come to think of as her own. Sitting sideways, she could look out over the lake toward the mountains on the other side, or back up the slope of lawn to Laurel Mountain's main lodge.

33

There were no other buildings on the lake; woods sloped down to the shore on the right and rock cliffs rose above the water on the left. Two long, low mountain ridges slanted down, meeting at the other end of the lake in the shape of a V, a single high peak rising symmetrically behind. Sometimes the lake was as still as a mirror, reflecting trees and mountains and rocks. Today, the sunlight glittered on wind-stirred ripples. Halfway across the lake Miranda could make out the silhouettes of a pair of diving birds, disappearing and reemerging in the golden shimmer.

Miranda did her best to pretend the sprawling log building with the many-windowed porch was just an ordinary lodge. That she was here for a long rest, just to soak up the soothing beauty of the place between semesters. And the safety. Laurel Mountain really could be a kind of refuge, she thought, watching the birds dive. News broadcasts were blacked out on the television sets. "Too disturbing for the patients," she'd been told when she asked about it. It was funny, she thought. The crazy kids here had to be protected from the news of the violent world the adults considered sane. The mountains that kept the patients in also kept the world out.

When, in spite of the insect repellent, the blackflies clustering near her eyes and whining in her ears got to be too much, she went inside, hoping to sit on the porch and keep her focus on the mountains. But the porch was the activity room, and as she came through the curtained French doors she saw it was busy. Children in paint-spattered smocks were sitting at low tables, sloshing finger paints across the white Formica tops. They had no paper.

A little girl at a nearby table began flinging yellow paint. Hurriedly, Miranda turned back toward the doors. As she did, she noticed a girl sitting at a separate table in the far corner, moving one hand into and out of three fat blobs of paint—one red, one blue, and one yellow. Unlike the others, who were slathering paint everywhere, this girl used her fingers as an artist would use a brush. She seemed totally absorbed, working quickly, without pausing to think or to examine what she had done. She dabbed a little of one color or a little of another and moved her hand—Miranda noticed it was her left hand—carefully, almost delicately.

Intrigued, Miranda moved closer. The girl had smooth, shiny black hair, clipped back with barrettes on either side of her face, and falling halfway down her back. Her skin was a soft café au lait color, and she was so small and thin inside her smock that Miranda thought she looked breakable, like a porcelain figure that should be kept behind glass. Everything about her except her left hand was concentrated, focused, still.

Miranda leaned to see what the girl was painting. When she saw, she gasped out loud. Using just those three colors, and without seeming to look up once, she had painted the scene outside the windows. There was the lawn and the line of white stones that marked the off-limits beach. Above that was the lake, the mountain at the end, and the blue sky above, white tabletop showing through in little fist marks of clouds.

The girl looked up. Her eyes, a vibrant, piercing green, met Miranda's and held. Miranda felt herself caught. Trapped. For a long moment, neither moved. Miranda felt the girl was looking not *at* her but somehow *into* her. She tried to look away but couldn't. She had a sense that the child, familiar somehow, was trying to tell her something. Something important. But she couldn't understand.

The art therapist, a young woman in a short-sleeved leotard

and a wraparound skirt, came toward them, and the spell was broken. The girl jerked around in her seat and began splatting the paint with both hands. By the time the therapist looked, the painting of the lake had vanished and the little table was covered, just like the tables where the other children were, with a mess of muddy color.

*June 9, 2000*_____

TARYN ALLOWED THE AIDE TO clean her hands and face with a big wet terry-cloth towel and then undo the Velcro fastening of the paint smock.

This was it. The change she had felt beyond the snow.

First had come the whisper of energy from the silent, rocking boy, telling her that he was only lost, only frightened, not broken like the others. Then the dream. And now the girl from the dream—Miranda. Taryn had felt her presence like warmth from a woodstove the moment she came through the doors. So she had dared to let her see the painting, dared, then, to *reach*. This time, for the first time in Taryn's life, she was sure the reaching had connected. Taryn felt her heart beating in her throat. She was certain now. The change she had been waiting for had begun.

*June 9, 2000*_____

ELIJAH SAT VERY STILL ON the hard planks of the floor. The room was blessedly quiet. No one thumped or bumped. No one cried or yelled. The big lodge had been noisy all the time—even at night, because the boy in the other bed had snored and snorted and sometimes screamed. Now even the low growl was gone—the growl that had lurked in Elijah's head behind all the other noises, the growl that rose or fell in the lodge but never stopped. It had dwindled behind him as they walked across the lawn and through the trees, fading and fading until, when the front door of this new place had swung shut, it vanished.

It was so quiet he could almost believe he was alone here, with the smell of new wood and furniture polish and the line of sunlight that lay across his feet. But Elijah could feel her presence, sense her breathing in the air behind him. Dr. Abigail sat on the couch, her sandaled feet on the Indian-patterned rug, a book open on her lap. From time to time, he heard the whisper of a page turning. "I have a few things to read, so I'll stay," she had told the man before he left. "He's no trouble."

No trouble. Elijah rested his chin on his knees, rubbing one finger around and around the rim of the empty wastebasket. He faced the knotty-pine corner of the room, but he did not look at the walls that met in front of him, ignored the animal faces looking out at him from the golden wood, their dark pine-knot eyes and noses snooping. He did not watch his finger moving along the comfortable circle. Around and around, with no surprises, no sharp angles or changes in direction. *No trouble.* This log house they had brought him to was the first place in his life where anyone would say he was no trouble.

When he and his mother and great-grandmother had come up to the city he had been trouble at school, rocking in his chair with his eyes closed, making stories, building their people and pictures in his mind through the long, noisy hours. They had talked, the teachers. Sometimes they had yelled. They had pushed books with a few words and flat, bright pictures in front of him. Or papers. They had wrapped his hand around a pencil. Sometimes he had done what they wanted him to do, said a word, made a few letters, drawn a picture; most times he had not. He discovered he could look at a person's face, right at the big eyes and nose and moving mouth, and not have to see them. Like going out from behind his eyes. One day he had stopped going to school, and nobody ever came to make him go back.

His great-grandmother, who had loved him, whose ample body and warm, comforting arms, whose smell of cinnamon and molasses he still missed every single day, had known from the start that he was trouble. Much as she had loved him, she had known. "Don't you let on you're readin', baby—hear? We just keep that a secret between us two. Gifts like you got scare people. And scared people turn mean. Mighty, mighty mean. Your mama was always a smart one, but not like you. She won't know what to do with you if she finds out. Won't *nobody* know what to do with you."

So no one had known that when Mama Effie sat on her chair on the porch reading Bible stories to him, even back then, when he was still in diapers, still sucking his thumb, he had read the words along with her. When they came to the city, she'd bring home books from the library, two at a time, hide them for him under his mattress.

The two of them had kept the other secret, too. The way he had always known when her feet were paining her or her back ached. The way she had known about his nightmares and would be there with him in the middle of the night, even before his grow-ing terror could make him scream, already touching his back, gen-tling him out of it.

There had been other secrets. Not even Mama Effie had known about him and his mother. The things he knew without her telling him. How he could feel the darkness rise in his own mind whenever she was scared. How he used to feel the tight, caged feeling that came to her so often and so strong.

Now Elijah stared down at the torn toe of his sneaker in the sunlight, the bit of sock showing. And felt his finger going around and around. It had all been for nothing. Mama Effie had been wrong. Silence and secrets had not made him safe. Had not kept Mama Effie from the hospital or from the sudden violent pain that shattered his sleep that awful night when he was six years old. The pain that, when it stopped, left an empty space inside and out.

And silence had not kept the angry man from moving into his world when his great-grandmother was gone. Secrets had not saved him from that man, who always thought of him as trouble. "Something wrong with this kid," the man had said, "something bad in his eyes. Looking all the time. Not talking. Look how he looks at me. I seen him looking at you that way, too. Crazy. You oughta do something with him. Send him somewhere."

The man had begun to hit him for looking. Kick him. Black his eyes sometimes. So Elijah had stopped looking. But it hadn't helped. His mother must have felt his pain at the beginning. Elijah caught her wincing sometimes at the blow. But the man turned on her then, too. And little by little the connection between Elijah and his mother had faded till it was just that last pale, thin thread.

The growl had begun then, the warning in his head that let him escape sometimes. But he couldn't get his mother to hear it. Couldn't save her.

All that long, cold night after she was gone, when he knew he was alone in the world, he had stayed beneath his bush, keeping his head filled with the soft white fog. They had found him the next day, the women who asked so many questions. He had looked at them without seeing them, closing his ears as best he could until the questions stopped. He had made a vow that night never to connect with people again. Never again.

Finally the women had brought him to the lodge. There had been no hiding place there, but he had huddled when he could in the corner of the big room, ignoring the people who tried to make him do things. Until he found the books.

And then the soft-voiced man with the white beard and the woman with the long gray hair, talking about family, had brought him here.

Elijah let his eyes focus on the wall for a moment. A golden fox face, tilted sideways, looked back at him from the pine board. A soft, quiet fox face that seemed to smile. Elijah looked away again, at the finger moving on the wastebasket rim.

Behind him a page turned with a whisper as Abigail Periodes read.

*June 9, 2000*_____
TRANSCRIPT, THERAPY SESSION
PATIENT: Miranda Ellenby
PRIMARY THERAPIST: Harlan Turnbull, M.D., Ph.D.

TURNBULL: Let's begin today with Paris. Okay?

MIRANDA: Yes.

TURNBULL: Good. Now, according to—[paper shuffling sound]—
Dr. Miriam Freidenberg...She was your adviser?

MIRANDA: Yes.

TURNBULL: According to Dr. Freidenberg, you were to meet her
for breakfast, but you left the hotel instead and did
not return until late afternoon the next day. Just
before you were due to present your paper.

MIRANDA: Yes.

TURNBULL: I know that you've never spoken publicly about the
time you were missing. I will not ask you at this
point to tell me what you did. I only need to know
something about your thoughts during that time.
And more importantly, your feelings. If you are
willing to acknowledge having feelings.

MIRANDA: Yes. [long silence]

TURNBULL: Miranda?

MIRANDA: Yes.

TURNBULL: You do remember that period, don't you?

MIRANDA: Yes.

TURNBULL: Good. Just start anywhere. What you were thinking
or feeling when you left the hotel, for instance?

MIRANDA: Yes. [long silence]

TURNBULL: [clears throat] Miranda?

MIRANDA: Yes.

TURNBULL: Oh. [pause] Oh, I get it. You've decided that the only
thing you're going to say today is yes.

MIRANDA: Yes.

TURNBULL: I see. Very cute.

MIRANDA: Yes.

TURNBULL: [long pause] Miranda, it is very clear to me that you think you're smarter than I am—

MIRANDA: Yes.

TURNBULL: Fine. Leaving aside the question of life experience, and the difficulty of defining human intelligence in terms of a score on a test, I am willing to concede that your intellectual machinery, if you will, is more powerful and probably more efficient than the intellectual machinery of anyone at this facility, including myself. However, you are here. And you are here not as a visiting dignitary, but as a patient. That ankle bracelet should be enough to remind you of your situation. An astronomical IQ does not make you impervious to psychosis, Miranda. Quite the contrary. I gather you feel certain you're not sick. That you don't belong here—

MIRANDA: Yes.

TURNBULL: But that's the trick, don't you see? You *are* here. The less sick you think you are, the more sick you show yourself to be. You're so proud of that mind of yours that you've built your whole world there. You live there like a hermit, never venturing out to make meaningful contact with regular people. You have many languages and no one with whom to communicate. [long silence] There's something not quite human about that, don't you see? Not normal. Not normal at all.

MIRANDA: I have never thought myself normal.

TURNBULL: Don't sneer at normalcy, Miranda. It's going to take
             a heavy dose of it to get you out of here. Understand
             this with that wonderful brain of yours—the only
             way for you to leave Laurel Mountain, the *only* way,
             is for me to say you're ready. Your parents have
             entrusted you to my care. Understand? [long silence]
             I'm here to help you. We can go about this the direct
             and simple way, with me asking questions and you
             answering them, so that I can structure a useful
             therapy. Or we can go about it in another way,
             where you will have no choice whatsoever. I am, as
             you know, a psychiatrist, a medical doctor. I have
             other tools in my black bag besides talk therapy.
             I gather, since you have such fine intellectual
             machinery, you understand me.

MIRANDA: Yes.

TURNBULL: Good. Shall we continue this session?

MIRANDA: No.

TURNBULL: All right. Now that you have something to think
             about, what you need is a nice quiet weekend to
             think. We'll begin again on Monday morning.

Journal—Miranda Ellenby
June 9, 2000—11:50 P.M.

**A hermit in my mind, Turnbull says! No contact with regular
people. Regular people! Where would I find any here? And even**

*if I found them, how would he define "meaningful" contact?
For me or for them? No regular people have ever wanted to
have contact with me before, unless I could do something for
them. Answer a question, translate something, perform for
them. And where does he get off talking about being "normal"?
As if anybody has ever even wanted me to be "normal." What a
cretin the man is!*

*Still, I underestimated him. That "psychiatrist as medical
doctor" business was a threat to use drugs, which probably
means Mother and Daddy didn't rule them out when they
brought me here. What could they have been thinking of? I
should have taken more than that survey course in abnormal
psych so I'd have a better idea what kinds of drugs they use in
a place like this. Not that it matters. They all mess with the
brain.*

NOT THIS BRAIN!

*I ought to be able to fool a shrink who took as long as that
to notice I was giving the same answer to every question he
asked. The library here doesn't have much of a collection of
great literature, but it has plenty of books about the ways the
human mind can get derailed. With a little research I ought to
be able to turn him into a pretzel trying to come up with a
diagnosis. I just need to be sure what I do doesn't suggest
heavy-duty drugs as a "useful therapy."*

*I can't seem too cooperative too fast, or he'll get suspicious.
He has to think he's tricking me into revealing the real me. I
could sneak in a characteristic of one thing here and another
there—a little manic depression, a touch of paranoia. Some
obsessive-compulsive behavior shouldn't be too hard. I could*

start washing my hands all the time. Or touching all the panes
in every window before I leave a room.

If I do this right, maybe I can drive HIM *crazy!*

June 10, 2000—9:00 P.M. _____

THE DARKNESS OF ELIJAH'S ROOM was softened, near the slightly
open door, by the glow from the hall. Shadows lay still around
him and Elijah lay in the middle, warm under his striped blanket,
feeling the quiet. For two days there had been no growling sound.
Elijah had begun to let himself look, and he had seen the books.
Shelves and shelves of books. He hadn't taken one yet, but he
probably could. Would. He had let himself look—really look—at
the man and the woman who lived here, too. They looked kind
enough. Dr. Noah, the man's name was. Noah.

Elijah knew the story of the Bible Noah. He and Mama Effie
had read it many times, and it was one of his favorites. It had a
happy ending, not like some in the Bible, not like Samson or Lot's
wife. Elijah liked happy endings best. Mama Effie did, too, but she
told him not to count on them, either in stories or in life. "There's
lots of happy in every life," she would say. "Only sometimes it's
small, and quick. You have to keep your eyes peeled so you don't
miss it."

You didn't have to keep your eyes peeled for the happy in the
Noah story, though. Elijah filled his mind with it and its pictures.
After the arkful of animals—every kind of animal and bird in the
world—had sailed on the waters for a long, long time, the water
finally began to go down. So Noah sent a raven out, to fly up and

45

down and look for land. And then he sent a dove. Most people remembered only the dove, Mama Effie had told him. "But Noah sent the raven first."

It was the dove, though, that brought back the olive leaf, so Noah knew the Flood had ended. Noah sailed the ark to a mountain that was sticking high out of the water, and Noah's family and all the animals moved down from the ark onto the dry land, two by two, to build their families and make a new world.

The best part was the promise God made never to flood the world and kill its people and its animals again. Rainbows were the sign of that promise—rainbows that made stripes in the sky like the stripes on Elijah's blanket.

Elijah yawned. He snuggled deeper under his covers and closed his eyes. The animals had been safe with Noah and his family. Maybe he would be safe here, with Dr. Noah and Dr. Abigail.

Behind his closed eyes, Elijah saw animals, two at a time—sheep and cows and gorillas and snakes—coming down from the big old boat. Then, for a moment, Mama Effie was there, and his mother, with a dove perched on her shoulder. His mother was smiling. A low growling sound began, and the dove flew away. The images grew jumbled and ran together.

Elijah felt himself rising. He felt air rushing past his face and knew that he was flying. He felt his arms moving up and down with slow, strong strokes. He turned his head and saw his wing feathers, black and gleaming. He looked down. He was high in the sky. Ahead of him, pale and distant, were the blue points of mountains. Far below him tall grass blew in wind patterns, like ocean waves. He stilled his wings, gliding on the air, letting it hold him up. Tipping, he began a long, slow circle. And heard the booming, like thunder. Saw bursts of light and flame on the horizon. Distant explosions. The growling in his head became a roar.

Then he saw, so far below him that they seemed to be toys, a horse and rider moving fast through the tall grass. Something white in front of the rider caught the light of the rising sun so brightly that he blinked. He completed his circle and beat his wings once, twice, staying with the figures that moved swiftly below him, away from the spreading flames.

June 11, 2000

AFTER DINNER SUNDAY AFTERNOON Miranda avoided the group of teenage patients who had clustered around the big television in the dayroom to watch a video. She was heading for the comfortable chair in the corner of the big living room, a textbook on child and adolescent psychology she had borrowed from the library in her hand, when she saw Polly Perky gathering the younger children and their aides for a nature walk. Taryn, the green-eyed girl, was standing quietly in the excited cluster of children, waiting her turn to be rubbed with insect repellent and sunscreen.

Since she had seen Taryn's painting, shared that moment of connection, Miranda had found herself watching the girl, drawn to what seemed to be a quiet, listening awareness, and to those eyes, which so often, when she wasn't staring out a window, watched her back. Taryn was constantly looking out—at trees, mountain, lake—as if the outdoors were a magnet, pulling on her. And she took every offer of a chance to go outside. Miranda couldn't decide whether the girl was desperate to escape or whether she was storing images for some future finger painting. When anyone from the staff was near, Taryn went blank, as if she didn't pay attention to anything, indoors or out. But Miranda had a strong sense that there wasn't anything Taryn *didn't* notice.

Now Taryn looked over at her, and Miranda felt again that she was trying to communicate something, sending some sort of signal that Miranda couldn't decipher.

"Come on the walk with us," a voice behind her said. She turned to see the short, sturdy-looking aide she had overheard complaining about a French class she was taking at the local community college. When Miranda had said to her, *"Parlez-vous français?"* the girl had made a face and answered with a heavy North Country accent, *"Oon pew,"* so Miranda had dubbed her Pew. No mental giant, at least Pew wasn't as bad as most. She didn't smile all the time or intersperse every phrase with a laugh, as if Laurel Mountain were some sort of television sitcom and she was there to provide the laugh track.

Now Pew leaned closer to her and whispered, "We have to take two patients each, but I've got Timmy the Terror, so I'll have my hands full." Her grin turned Miranda into an ally. "If you'll come along and be my second, I'll owe you one." Miranda grinned back, feeling absurdly pleased, and nodded. Polly Perky was organizing the group into a line now, with Taryn's threesome at the front.

"We'll bring up the rear," Pew told Polly Perky, and took a firm hold of Timmy's hand. The boy tried to pull free, but Pew just smiled at him, her grip tightening. "It's like a trail ride," she told Miranda. "Always put the horse that kicks last." On cue, Timmy aimed a kick at Pew's ankle. Nimbly, she stepped aside.

Pew leaned closer to him. "If you watch carefully enough on our walk," she said, her voice conspiratorial, "and stay very, very quiet, you just might see a mountain troll. But they disappear if you holler or try to chase them. Disappear into thin air!" She winked at Miranda as they followed the line of children outside.

Their route took them across the lawn and around the end of the lake to the right of the lodge, onto a wide bark-mulched trail that led under the trees. Though the sun was bright overhead and the air was still and summery warm, when they moved under the trees the light was dimmer, the air noticeably cooler. At the front of the line Polly Perky was calling out the names of trees and pointing out mushrooms and mosses, but few of the children were paying attention. This was less like a nature walk, Miranda decided, than a circus parade. The aides had to keep herding children back to the path or snatching them off boulders they had scurried away to climb. There was no chance for anything like conversation. Pew was so busy trying to keep Timmy from stomping to death every plant or wildflower or fungus within a yard of the path that she had no time or breath for talk.

The path began angling upward, away from the lake, and soon Miranda felt sweat trickling down her sides beneath her T-shirt. She had just decided to ask Pew whether she could go back to the lodge when Polly Perky, looking considerably less perky than usual, called a rest break. They were in an area studded with boulders, through which wound a thin stream, gurgling over mossy rocks. Almost immediately, children were clambering onto boulders or splashing the shallow water with hands or feet, shouting with glee.

Timmy pulled himself free of Pew's clutches and, shouting

about mountain trolls, plunged uphill toward a tall outcropping of rock with a dark opening that looked like a cave. Pew went after him. Any self-respecting mountain troll would be miles away by now, Miranda thought, as she sat down on a rock, glad of a chance to catch her breath and rest her weary legs. She was not used to this much physical activity. For a long time, she watched the mob of children and aides until she realized that Taryn wasn't among them.

She looked around and saw her, only a few yards away, standing utterly still beside the narrow trunk of a tree, her eyes closed, a hand pressed to the tree's bark on either side. As Miranda watched, tears leaked from beneath the girl's tightly closed eyelids and slid down her cheeks.

As if the commotion around them had suddenly stopped, Miranda felt herself encased in a bubble of stillness. At the center were Taryn and the tree. It was, she saw, some kind of short-needled fir. Its bottom branches were brown and dry, the ones above beginning to turn yellow. Only at the very top were the needles the dark green color of the other trees. A thick line of oozing, sticky sap ran down the rough bark between Taryn's hands.

Taryn took a deep breath and began to move her hands gently on the trunk, as if she were stroking an animal. After a long moment, she leaned her forehead against the rough bark, continuing the movement of her hands more slowly now. Miranda became aware of an ache, all through her legs and up to her chest. It was different from the tiredness of her muscles from the walk, sharper and more insistent. Then she became aware of a deep, inexplicable sadness. Her vision blurred as tears welled.

She discovered she was holding her breath. As she breathed in,

Polly Perky blew her whistle, and the noise of the children washed over her again. Whatever the spell had been, the whistle had broken it. Miranda felt perfectly normal again. She blinked away the tears and gave her head a shake. Taryn's aide, holding the hand of Todd, a boy who never seemed aware of anything except his fingers, which he constantly twiddled in front of his eyes, bustled up and snatched at Taryn's arm. "Let's go!" the aide said as Taryn moved out of reach. "We have to stay at the head of the line."

Taryn, her hands still on the tree, turned her green eyes on Miranda with the intensity of a laser beam. Her lips did not move, but Miranda had a sense as clear as if Taryn had spoken out loud. *It's dying.*

Just then a shriek from Timmy split the air, and Taryn's aide, pulling Todd behind her, went to help Pew pull him down from the tree he was attempting to climb.

Miranda dug a Kleenex out of the pocket of her shorts and took it to Taryn. The girl smiled. When she had blown her nose and wiped her face, she stuffed the tissue into the back pocket of her jeans and pulled out a tightly folded paper.

"Taryn!" her aide called. "Let's go!"

She slipped the paper into Miranda's hand and hurried away. Miranda started to unfold it, then changed her mind and put it in her pocket. Pew was crouched beside Timmy, holding him by both arms and talking to him intently. Miranda looked back at the tree and knew, absolutely knew, that it was true. It was dying, its life force draining away, its cells shutting down. Feeling like a fool, she laid her hand against the sticky bark.

I'm sorry, she thought at it. I'm really sorry. And seemed to feel a small shudder under her hand.

51

Tale of a Dreamer

> *They said I was a prophet.*
> *I heard voices that no other heard*
> *And saw things that none other glimpsed.*
> *Men flocked to me when I walked by*
> *Holding communion with myself.*
> *"You are a prophetess!" they cried. "Prophesy to us!*
> *You are a prophet!"*
> > *Weary, weeping*
> *World-worn, I went on my way*
> > *Wary into the wild world-night.*

> *They said I was mad*
> *I heard voices that no other heard*
> *And saw things that none other glimpsed.*
> *Men drew away when I walked by*
> *Holding communion with myself.*
> *"She is a madwoman!" they cried. "Drive her away!*
> *She is mad!"*
> > *Weary, weeping*
> *World-worn, I went on my way*
> > *Wary into the wild world-night.*

> *Still I, a mad and dreaming prophet*
> *Hear things that no other hears*
> *And see things that none other glimpses.*
> *Men pay me no mind when I walk by*

Holding communion with myself.
Nothing say they of me, nothing they ask
And I am left alone, a mad and dreaming prophetess.
  Still
  Weary, weeping
World-worn, I go on my way
  Wary into the wild world-night.

Journal—Miranda Ellenby
June 11, 2000—4:00 P.M.

A kid's printing and the letter T at the bottom. For Taryn. She can't be more than nine or ten. But she wrote the poem, I'm sure of it! Incredible. What else can this kid do?

"Wary into the wild world-night." As I read it I got goose bumps on the back of my neck. Wild world-night. I remembered, suddenly, the soldiers on Paris streets. The police on campus—no safe place. Everywhere, after dark, the wild world-night.

The goose bumps are back as I type this. I know why she seems so familiar. Those eyes. She's the cat in my dream.

So what does she prophesy, this kid with the cat's eyes? And did she—did she?—make me feel the pain of that dying tree?

If I AM an alien, I think I've finally met another one.

LAUREL MOUNTAIN CENTER FOR RESEARCH AND REHABILITATION

PATIENT NUMBER	LAST NAME FIRST NAME M.I.	DATE ADMITTED	
4978	Forrester, Taryn M.	3/6/99	

LEGAL STATUS AT ADMISSION	AGE	SEX	RACE
Involuntary	9y, 1m	F	Mixed

HOME ADDRESS	EDUCATIONAL STATUS AT ADMISSION	CITY & STATE OF BIRTH
Rt. 3, Box 53 Middleton Springs, VT 05757	Home-schooled	Middleton Springs, VT

FATHER'S NAME	ADDRESS PHONE	OCCUPATION
"Raptor"	(unknown)	Itinerant poet, songwriter

MOTHER'S MAIDEN NAME	ADDRESS PHONE	OCCUPATION
Marian Forrester	(deceased)	(N/A)

PARENTS' MARITAL STATUS	PERSON TO NOTIFY IN EMERGENCY PHONE	RELATIONSHIP
(N/A)	Barbara Gale 802-555-0883	Aunt

ESTABLISHED DIAGNOSIS	DIAGNOSTIC IMPRESSION AT ADMISSION
None	Extremely withdrawn. Severely depressed, possibly hallucinatory. Schizophrenic tendencies? Unusual case.

ADDITIONAL NOTES REGARDING ADMISSION INTERVIEW

Though child does not respond readily, and not at all to factual questions, when she does respond, her speech is amazingly mature—unsettlingly so. Aunt provided virtually all known information. The child's father was a self-styled "performance artist" of indeterminate race and background (dark-skinned and dark-eyed) who disappeared shortly after the child's birth. The mother built an almost cultlike following—"The Church of St. Taryn," as the aunt calls it—around what she believed to be the child's mystical qualities, which the aunt claims were hallucinations. Mother killed in car accident 11/98. Child has lived with aunt and four male cousins since.

PREVIOUS HOSPITALIZATION	INSTITUTION	DATES: FROM TO	
None			

ADMITTING PHYSICIAN	SIGNATURE	DATE	
John Devereux	*John Devereux*	3/6/99	

"SO—WHAT DO YOU THINK?" Abigail Periodes asked her husband after the staff meeting as they walked along the path from the lodge to their new log home.

"About what?" Noah asked.

Abigail poked her elbow into his ample stomach. "You know perfectly well what—who. Taryn Forrester. You heard Marian's report."

Noah gave her an injured look and rubbed the spot she had poked. "Some report! I wouldn't believe a word of it if I didn't know how careful a researcher and how good a reading specialist Marian is."

"I know we'd planned to give Elijah more time to settle in before bringing in another child, but don't you think we should make Taryn number two? Now?"

"Does she fit the criteria?" Noah asked. "Being able to tell a book of poetry from a book of prose just by holding them in her hands suggests the child has some sort of psychic ability, not extreme intelligence. Hardly the same thing."

"Who says she couldn't have both?"

"What's your evidence? We don't know for certain she can even read—the regular way."

Abigail swung the canvas bag she was carrying at a swarm of insects hovering in a sunny spot above the path. "Did you pay attention to *what* poetry Marian offered her? Frost, Whitman, Dickinson, for heaven's sake! Cummings, Millay, T. S. Eliot! And a few volumes of children's poetry. The more challenging the material, the longer she held it! She had to be 'reading' it somehow, not just feeling the shapes of the poems on the page."

"Did her mother claim psychic reading as one of her mystical abilities? Along with the direct connection to God and whatever else?"

"I don't think we ever heard the whole story about what Taryn's mother said about her. The aunt not only didn't believe any of it, she was hostile, especially about the so-called direct connection to God. She called her Saint Taryn." Abigail shook her head. "Think what it must have been like when her mother died, for the child to suddenly find herself living with a woman for whom everything about her and the life she'd led was a threat. Plus four big, rowdy boys who tormented her. She couldn't hide her racial mix, but she must have wanted to hide anything else that made her differences obvious."

Noah kicked a stick out of the path. "Still, there's no proof of exceptional intelligence. No test scores, no school grades, no nothing! When her aunt tried to put her in school the whole thing was a disaster."

"Of course there aren't any scores. Taryn's mother had never let educators anywhere near her. The aunt said her sister had always been 'a little on the strange side,' but after she met Taryn's father, she 'went around the bend,' and after he disappeared, she started telling 'wild stories' about what her wonder baby could do. Like speaking in full sentences at six months."

"Wild stories that you think might have been true."

"Well, why not? There are documented cases of language that early. And sensing what's in a closed book by holding it in your hands *is* wild. Everyone was so ready to believe the aunt when she brought Taryn here. Maybe it's the mother's stories we should have paid attention to, what we have of them."

They had reached the newly completed log house now and mounted the steps to the broad front porch. "Elijah's still at the pool, isn't he?" Noah said.

"Tippy's bringing him over when his session is done."

"Good. And we don't have to start dinner yet." Noah settled himself heavily into one of the two Adirondack chairs that faced the view through the trees to the lakeshore. He picked up the newspaper that lay on the table between the chairs and set it in his lap, unopened. "Sit! Relax! Enjoy our new home."

Abigail put her bag on the table and sat with a sigh. "Okay, okay." She leaned back and took a long, slow breath, gazing up into the green tops of the towering pines that surrounded the house, listening to the wind among the branches.

After a few moments, Noah spoke. "What's most interesting to me in Marian's report is the time Taryn reacted so intensely to the batch of books Marian was taking back to the library for her son."

"The ones she hadn't intended to make part of the experiment."

Noah nodded. "Marian focused on the fact that Taryn had such a powerful reaction to books that were just sitting at the end of the table in a bag—books Taryn hadn't even touched. It hadn't occurred to her to think about content—what the books were. But I asked her after the meeting."

Abigail looked over at him. "So you *have* been thinking about this!"

"Of course I've been thinking about it."

She sighed. "So? What books were they?"

"Marian's son is a horror-fiction fan. That's what they all were—horror novels."

Abigail sat up. "Taryn didn't just reject those, she knocked them clear off the table."

"And refused to do anything else that session." Noah tapped his fingers on the arm of his chair. "Blood and terror. I have this mental picture of the images, the feelings from those books leaking out of them."

"Like toxic chemicals from a rusting storage drum."

"And Taryn picking them up." The two psychologists looked at each other for a moment.

"Whatever Taryn has, it's extreme," Abigail said. "And if she really *did* begin speaking at six months—"

"Okay, okay, I agree with you. If our point is to put children with extraordinary minds together, Taryn belongs." Noah scratched at his beard. "Besides, if we make her number two, we give ourselves some more time before we need to confront Harlan about Miranda Ellenby."

Abigail smiled. "My thought exactly. If we wait long enough, he may be just as glad to have an excuse to get rid of her. You can tell she's giving him trouble, though he'd die before he'd admit it."

"Of course, she could do the same with us," Noah said, grinning. "Are you up to handling the Phenom of the Century?"

"A wounded kid is a wounded kid. All we can do is remember Gordon Stephenson, put the kids together, and trust the concept."

"Not a lot of choice. We've more or less based the rest of our careers on it!" Noah shook out the newspaper and scanned the front-page headlines. "Look at this! 'Terrorist Bomb Kills Ninety-three in Barcelona.' I don't know why I bother reading the paper. It gets worse every day."

Journal—Miranda Ellenby
June 13, 2000—6:10 A.M.

Another dream! This one began exactly where the other one left off. It was just after dawn, and I was riding with the white cat in front of me on the saddle and the raven flying high above us. Behind us, seeming to get closer, was a kind of steady booming. Not thunder this time. Guns. Or bombs. I was scared and kept kicking the horse to go faster. There was no place to hide, and I felt terribly vulnerable. There was something I was supposed to be doing, some kind of mission. But I didn't know exactly what it was. Only that it was important. Like a quest. For what seemed a long time, we galloped across the open plain alongside a shallow river as the sun rose higher in the sky and the booming went on behind us. Finally we came to a line of trees that marked the beginning of a forest. The trail led in under the trees, and I could see that it was dark in there. The horse slowed to a walk. The trees would give us cover, but the forest might have dangers of its own. I looked up into the sky. The raven was still above us, riding a current of air in circles that grew wider as we hesitated.

I reined in the horse, and he stopped, stamping his hooves and taking little side steps. "You want to go?" I asked him, half-expecting an answer. He just strained at the bit and stamped.

I loosened the reins. The horse had been choosing the way so far—I decided to let him go on. But I wasn't sure I liked it. As the horse began to move forward again, I stroked the cat's head and felt the vibration of her purring. It made me feel better somehow. The air was cooler under the trees.

I pulled the sweater the old woman had given me closer and strained to hear any sounds that might mean danger. The booming had faded into the distance, and everything was quiet. When I did hear a sound, it came from above. I looked and saw the raven settling onto a high branch a little way ahead. It watched as we approached, turning its head as we walked underneath. Wherever we were going, it seemed, the raven was going, too.

Finally, I saw a glitter ahead and to the left. As we got closer, I could see that the trail was curving toward the shore of a lake. I was glad to be getting out of the woods.

Then I heard the sound of an ax against wood. And smelled smoke. The horse stepped out from under the trees, and I saw a lean-to set up between the forest and the sandy beach of the lake. I pulled the horse to a stop. A campfire burned in front of the lean-to, and ferns and pine boughs were piled beneath its shelter, making a soft-looking bed. A gray horse, head drooping, was tethered to a sapling. The ring of the ax sounded from farther down the beach. There seemed to be only one person camped here, but there was no way to tell if it was friend or foe.

We had been in the woods longer than I'd thought. The sun was slipping down the sky, tinting the clouds and the smooth surface of the lake a deep rose. Night would be falling soon, *and we had nowhere to go ourselves. Then I saw on a rock near the campfire a carved wooden whistle. I recognized the pattern; it was the whistle the old man had been carving.*

Before I could decide what that might mean, the cat leapt to the ground, its white fur tinted pink in the sunset glow. The raven glided down from a tree and landed on the top of the lean-to. The sound of the ax stopped. The raven lifted off and flew along the lakeshore, in the direction the sound had been coming from. I stayed where I was, ready to run.

That's when I woke up.

Tuesday, 6/13
Patient #5042 / Miranda Ellenby

Ellenby case is complex—intriguing. Isolation this intense could be a kind of psychosis in itself.

Though still highly resistant, patient is no longer playing mind games.

Initially patient denied dreaming. When pushed resorted to intellectual defense—a lengthy discourse on Jungian dream interpretation.

Indirect approach led to a reluctant description of intense recurring nightmare of being lost in labyrinthine cave. Stress evident during dream description—shivering, extreme restlessness, rapid blinking.

This first breach in patient's defenses has allowed other symptoms to surface. Signs of obsessive-compulsive behavior evident 6/12 and again today, though patient attempts to hide them. Touches windowpanes while apparently wandering aimlessly, giving rambling answers to simple questions. Wipes hands on shorts after each touch. Draws out sessions each day (in various ways) until each pane has been touched.

Patient asks repeatedly about "rules." Intense need for (aversion to?) structure?

Though patient interacts little with patients her age, she has begun to participate in some scheduled activities. Writes at length each day on the computer in her room (journal? diary?).

To Do
Research language patient uses when writing on computer in room—find translator.

Local Vandal Taken Into Custody

The youth allegedly responsible for the worst single incident of vandalism in this county's history was arrested this morning at his home.

Throughout Jay and Upper Jay, windshields of more than twenty cars were smashed June 13 in an apparently random pattern. Windows in several stores, including McAllister's Hardware, Smith's Sporting Goods and Guns, and two liquor stores, were shattered and inventory damaged during the rampage. Total damage estimates exceed $50,000.

The suspect, whose name is being withheld at the request of his family, pending trial, is a recent high school dropout. He has no police record, but as a freshman, he was allegedly suspended for hacking his way into the school's computer. Said by neighbors to be a loner, he appears to have been acting alone on Tuesday night. Police refuse to say whether drugs or alcohol were involved in the incident.

Bond has been set at $50,000.

Journal—Miranda Ellenby
June 15, 2000—10:15 P.M.

What I noticed first were the bandages on his wrists. That can mean only one thing here. He didn't hide them, which he might

have done by rolling down the sleeves of his shirt. But it wasn't as if he was trying to show them off, either. He just didn't seem to notice them. He moved through the food line in front of me, his shoulders hunched under the faded denim of his shirt. Tensed. Edgy. He looked—I don't know—hunted maybe. Like a wolf who's been caught, and injured, in a trap. Messed-up but still dangerous.

His black crew cut reminded me of when I shaved my head and it was starting to grow back. I wondered if the hair was a statement. Or what was left of a statement. Or just a haircut.

I can't be sure how old he is, but somewhere near me. Not eighteen, or he wouldn't be here. There was a faint line of beard shadow along his jaw and his upper lip. Blue eyes, intense as a torch flame. He's tall, over six feet, and lean, with a hard edge to him, wearing jeans and a denim shirt with the sleeves rolled up.

The only other guys near my age here are either so dulled out on meds that they look like zombies or so weird that you want to stay as far away as possible. This one is something else.

When he had his food, he stood for a minute, looking around. There's no place to sit alone, or I'm sure he would have found it. For one brief second I considered sitting at the table he chose. I remember what my first dinner here was like. Which is partly why I didn't sit there after all. I figured Tookie, who was just behind me, would do that. Florence says she does it with everybody new. The other reason was that, intrigued as I was, he scared me a little.

Sitting with Tookie isn't the worst way to begin here, probably—it makes you face right away how bad it's going to be. You can't pretend it's school or camp or something normal, with Tookie giggling and talking that half-comprehensible chatter of hers and reaching over to touch you all the time, as if she's trying to convince herself you're real and not some hallucination. I pushed her hand away every time she did it to me.

The first time she did it to him he ignored her, as if he didn't feel it, even though she left a smear of butterscotch pudding on his cheek. He just kept his head down and did his best to cut his mystery-meat patty with his bendy plastic fork. But when she did it again he stood up so suddenly that he knocked his chair over. Then he threw down his fork and stalked out of the cafeteria, those white bandages beaming their message to anybody who had enough brain cells left to interpret it.

LAUREL MOUNTAIN CENTER FOR RESEARCH AND REHABILITATION

PATIENT NUMBER	LAST NAME FIRST NAME M.I.	DATE ADMITTED	
5043	**McAllister, Douglas A.**	**6/15/00**	

LEGAL STATUS AT ADMISSION	AGE	SEX	RACE
Involuntary	**17y, 2m**	**M**	**W**

HOME ADDRESS	EDUCATIONAL STATUS AT ADMISSION	CITY & STATE OF BIRTH
Box 0025 Star Route Upper Jay, NY 12987	**Gr. 11**	**Plattsburgh, NY**

FATHER'S NAME	ADDRESS PHONE	OCCUPATION
John Lawrence McAllister	**Box 0025 Star Route Upper Jay, NY 12987 518-555-2161**	**Owner/manager, hardware store**

MOTHER'S MAIDEN NAME	ADDRESS PHONE	OCCUPATION
Claire Geroux	**(see above)**	**Clerk/bookkeeper, hardware store**

PARENTS' MARITAL STATUS	PERSON TO NOTIFY IN EMERGENCY PHONE	RELATIONSHIP
M	**John or Claire McAllister 518-555-2161**	**Parents**

ESTABLISHED DIAGNOSIS	DIAGNOSTIC IMPRESSION AT ADMISSION
Clinical depression	**Severe depression; subject slashed wrists with hunting knife the night after being arrested for an alleged vandalism spree involving the destruction of cars and shop windows, including his father's hardware store and the cars of his father and older brothers.**

ADDITIONAL NOTES REGARDING ADMISSION INTERVIEW

Subject stopped attending school in the fall of 1999; he finished high school math in seventh grade and claims there is nothing left for him in school—"or anywhere else." Refused to discuss vandalism, suicidal ideation, suicide attempt, or feelings.

PREVIOUS HOSPITALIZATION	INSTITUTION	DATES: FROM TO	
None			

ADMITTING PHYSICIAN	SIGNATURE	DATE	
Harlan Turnbull	*Harlan Turnbull*	**6/15/00**	

DOUG MCALLISTER SAT WHERE NOAH Periodes had left him, in a big leather chair, elbows on knees, head bent as if his neck couldn't bear the weight of it, staring past the bandages on his wrists at the worn Oriental rug. "Stay there as long as you want: just don't miss lunch," the therapist had said before he left the office. "Be here again on Monday—same time. You might feel more like talking by then." And he was gone.

"Why?" the earnest Santa Claus–looking guy had asked. Such a simple question. And he'd asked it nothing like the cops, who had treated Doug like Jack the Ripper, as if his great crime had been rape and murder instead of property damage. It didn't matter how anyone asked. He couldn't answer.

He had wanted a way out of a world that never wanted him in the first place, a world that had closed in so hard, he couldn't breathe. Maybe that was one way—maybe he'd taken the tire iron to all that glass to bash a hole he could breathe through.

He didn't know what had happened to him. Only that the old protections, the old way of making himself a place, had quit working. He could pinpoint when it started—the September day Mr. Garrety announced that symphonic band was one of the extras being canceled so the school could pay for a metal detector. Take away music to stop guns at the door! As if it mattered to keep guns out of school, when they waited in pickup trucks in the parking lot, at home in closets, under pillows. Guns everywhere, and no music. He had quit school the very next day.

Everything had crumbled after that, like a house of cards collapsing in slow motion. When it was over, standing in the rubble that had been his life, he'd seen himself for the coward he was. Had always been. He'd lived their way because he couldn't take the consequences of living his own. Even now the rage made his hands shake.

He had meant to use his deer rifle on everyone in his life who lived by the fist and the gun and power built on fear.

It must have been the logical fallacy that made him pick up the tire iron instead, smash property instead of lives. Trying to free himself from them with a gun, he would have proven himself, finally, irrevocably, one of them. Or was that just an excuse he was using to protect himself? That, too, like the rest of his life, cowardice? He couldn't sort it out anymore—which was their way and which was his.

He had even chickened out on chickening out. Doug closed his eyes, remembering the hunting knife, the blood oozing because he hadn't cut deep enough to make it sure.

But it wasn't pain that had stopped him. And it wasn't blood. Something else. Something.

Doug looked up at the clock on the wall behind Noah Periodes's desk. Lunch was nearly over. He stood up. Better here than jail, he supposed. No guns. Not even the television news to remind him. The hand beneath a bandaged wrist reached for the doorknob. Why? His own question was not the doctor's. Not why had he meant to die, but why had he chosen to live?

Journal—Miranda Ellenby
June 17, 2000—6:50 A.M.

Heard a flute in the middle of the night last night. I was sitting up in bed reading, and I had to stop and put down the book and just listen. It wasn't somebody playing Rampal or Galway on CD. It was real, starting and stopping. Improvisation, from the way it sounded. The melody was—I don't know exactly— haunting and lonely. Most of all lonely.

The music twined its way into me somehow. Like nothing I've ever heard before. Almost as if I recognized it. Not the notes, the melody, but the feeling.

Listening to it I felt as if I was on top of a mountain, in the cold, cold wind, all alone except for scrub and wildflowers and granite, seeing the whole world spread out in patterns of green and gold and blue, knowing that I couldn't reach it or touch it. I couldn't tell where music left off and images began.

I must have drifted to sleep, because I jolted awake again, and it was perfectly quiet and my reading light hurt my eyes. I turned it off and put my book on the bedside table. Moonlight lay in pale diamonds on the nubby blanket, and I lay for a long time, wishing the music would come again.

Clouds chase across a woven field of rain
As the wind bows the treetops slowly to the earth.
Amidst the curtain-web of rain across the centuries
A little girl stands looking at the world.
She isn't sure quite yet if she belongs here.

She wonders where she was before she came, and how
*   it was she arrived.*
If she fell to the earth-mother's breast like a falling star,
*   burning the heavens with*
A gentle light
If she grew rooted out of the earth, and severed
*   her roots—*
She wonders if the roots really are cut.
Her toes dig deeper into the soft deep mud.
She looks up into the clouds and sees the stars behind
*   her eyes.*

Around her is an alien world she has lived in lifelong
Peering like a bird into the windows.
Around her guns are sounding far away.
The soil has been reddened by untimely blood.
The stars are invisible to most people during the day
And even to her except in little glimpses that chase
*   around the corners of her soul.*
The raindrops water her—her toes dig deeper.
She relaxes as a plant stretches for the rain.
There is a gleam of star-dust in her eyes.

TARYN, CROSS-LEGGED ON THE BED, put down her pencil and reread the poem she had written. She took a deep breath and gazed around the room her new doctors had said would be her own. Her own. No other bed here, no broken child whose nightmares would fill the darkness with monsters. Like a plant moved into a new garden, she knew she could root herself here.

She stroked the white-dotted coverlet on the bed. The warm gold of the walls comforted her. The window faced away from the lodge, giving her a view of the woods. Outside, beyond the rain-streaked pane, old, dark trees and upstart vines and scrub and saplings were a still, comforting presence.

On a shelf above the bed were books, all poetry. She had run her hands over them, feeling her heart beat faster as the images flew past, some of them familiar from the books her mother had given her.

Mother. A flash of pain brought sudden tears. Life with her mother seemed so long ago now that sometimes it felt no more real than her own poetry, no more than images, caught in time, slipping further and further away. Her mother and the people who had come for answers, or healing, or sometimes just to watch her work, the way they would watch a magician, looking for the tricks. And the flicker of fear in their eyes when they could find no tricks. Sometimes the same flicker in her mother's eyes.

Since then there had been insistent realities—Aunt Barbara and the taunting cousins, the battleground of school. And then the lodge, with its layers of turmoil bubbling always underneath. Those realities had pushed her to hide, to watch, to listen and imitate, taking on protective coating, making herself invisible as she tried not to notice the growing darkness she could feel pressing in from the world outside.

Taryn's eyes stopped their slow movement around the room, caught by the orange clay pot that held an African violet in full bloom, the frilly pink flowers delicate and cheerful against the dark furry leaves. It smiled, welcomed. Taryn smiled back.

These people, Noah and Abigail Periodes, were different. Until they'd brought her here, they had only been part of the Laurel Mountain Center, more people she had to fool. Now she understood they, too, were part of the change. They had made a place for her, and for the others—a safe place.

This house was part of it, too. It felt familiar, as if she'd been here before, in this room of her own, with its smiling violet, its smell like the deep woods. Bed, dresser, desk, mirror, closet. Curtains at the window to match the coverlet. White towel and washcloth hanging on the back of the door. Dr. Abigail had shown her the bathroom at the end of the hall. It was new, shiny, clean. "Girls will share," she had said. Girls. Would Miranda be coming?

Taryn closed her eyes. And felt the presence of the other child nearby. Elijah. He was moving now, as he always used to move in his corner in the lodge, rocking and protected. But he was not shut down as hard as he had been before. A shaft of feeling, like light through a widening crack, leaked out. Taryn nodded to herself.

In the kitchen Dr. Abigail was moving around, opening cupboards, clattering dishes. Dr. Noah was there, too, moving more slowly. Two solid presences—familiar, like the house.

Taryn took a deep breath and let her mind slip sideways, out into the wet stillness under the trees.

Journal—Miranda Ellenby
June 22, 2000—11:40 p.m.

Interesting term for a psychiatrist—shrink: "to become reduced in amount or value, to dwindle; to cause to shrink." I like the Old English term GESCRUNCEN. *Fits Turnbull somehow. He tries to make me smaller so he can feel bigger. The tactic of a small, scared man. Hiding out up here in the boondocks with a bunch of sick kids he can have power over.*

When you look at Turnbull, he smiles. Always smiles. But when he thinks no one is looking it all slips, as if millions of microscopic rubber bands under the skin of his face let go and everything sags.

```
Hello.
?????
Repeat—Hello!
```
I didn't type those words. They just appeared on my screen.
```
To answer, type "!talk lab1" (without the quotes) and then type
your answer. That puts you in interactive mode. A hard return will
end transmission—like saying "Over" on a radio system.
```
!talk lab1 Who's there? How'd you get into my system?
```
Good—plain English. What was that before, code?
```
None of your business. How'd you get into my system?
```
If you don't know about interactive mode, you must not be one of
them.
```
Them?
```
Staff. They use interactive mode to communicate between
departments. I'm not in your system. We're both in theirs.
```

Who are you?

All lodge terminals are connected to a central memory. Your stuff is coming in, but it's all gobbledygook.

What do you mean my stuff is coming in?

Big Brother's watching. When you log in with your password all your stuff gets saved to the main memory—every ten minutes. Your last save was less than five minutes ago.

You didn't answer me. Who are you?

Who are *you*? You log on mostly late at night, so I took a chance you weren't staff.

I asked first. Who are you? Where are you?

Figure it out. "lab1." Computer lab terminal 1.

The computer lab's supposed to be locked at night.

Who said it isn't? I just said I'm in here. ;-)

WHO ARE YOU?

An inmate.

How'd you get into a locked lab?

Don't ask. You're an inmate, too?

Yes.

Name?

Why should I give you my name? You haven't said yours.

Doug. Yours?

Miranda.

Ellenby? That explains the gobbledygook. I heard you were here. What language was that?

Not one anybody else can read.

Smart.

Doug. That doesn't tell me anything.

You'll remember the wrists.

Oh.

Oh.

How do I know that's who you are? All I can see is words on my screen.

You *can't* know for sure. Any more than I can know you're really Miranda Ellenby.

You could be one of the shrinks trying to trick me into writing in English.

A shrink wouldn't warn you about central memory.

You might. You'd have nothing to lose, since I was already writing in a language you couldn't read. You might just be trying to gain my trust so I'd talk.

Don't you talk in your sessions?

That's between me and Turnbull.

Turnbull—the peeled grape?

Peeled grape! That's good. Who's yours?

Periodes.

Him or her?

Him. You don't find the Grape a big help?

I don't need help.

Oh, right. Let me guess—life was great and all was well between you and the world when your parents just suddenly up and dumped you here.

At least I didn't try to kill myself.

Who says I did? How hard do you think it really is to find an artery? Anyway, whether you tried or not depends on your definition, doesn't it?

What's that supposed to mean?

76

Miranda Ellenby. If I remember the story, you did tell the whole world you're an alien.

So?

Are you saying that had nothing to do with your being here? Not even the old "abducted by aliens" story—you had to claim you *were* one. The general term for such a claim is, pardon the expression, crazy. Not a great way to keep your old "Phenom of the Century" life going.

Listen, you broke into my system, I didn't break into yours.

Go away.

What you said was you don't need help. If you believe you're an alien, maybe you're having just the smallest bit of trouble distinguishing between fantasy and reality.

Who says I believed it?

Then why say it? It got you here, right? Not so smart for Miranda Ellenby, Baby Genius.

I'm not a baby. I'm 16.

There's still the genius part.

I hate that word.

Why?

If people started calling you that when you were three, you'd know.

Maybe they did. Maybe I do.

What?

Not three, actually. More like five. The school psychologist caught me in kindergarten, before I knew how much I had to hide in school. It's not the word my family uses, though. Did you honestly believe you were the only phenom on the planet? Not that the species seems to have much brain going for it in general. I'd bet on dolphins over us any day. Ever see a dolphin with a bomb?

That's just the sort of thing you'd say if you were a shrink
trying to get a rise out of me.

I'm not a shrink.

Prove it.

How about I sit with you at lunch in the cafeteria tomorrow. Unless you'd planned to sit with some other madman.

That's tomorrow.

Best I can do.

You mentioned my password before. I don't have a password. At
least I've never had to enter one.

I assume you're on a terminal in your room.

Yes.

Then the password must get entered automatically when you turn it on. They'd need to label your stuff so they know it when they find it. I'm telling you, they do the whole Big Brother thing. Not very well, but they try.

I thought I had a whole machine to myself.

Just what they wanted you to think. All the better to see your innermost thoughts. Except that you screwed them by writing those thoughts in—what language?

Muktuluk.

That ought to teach them to mess with geniuses. Muktuluk. Is that some obscure Eskimo dialect? Languages aren't my thing.

I made it up. Like Tolkien did with Elvish, only mine uses the
Roman alphabet.

I gather I'm supposed to be impressed.

You don't happen to know anything about wolves, do you?
Wolves?

Never mind. What IS your thing?
Tire irons.

?

In-joke. Guns, hunting knives, tire irons—North Country male,
that's me. Ask anybody.

North Country male genius?
So I'm an oxymoron, too. Nice paradox, don't you think?
Moron/genius. Actually, I don't have *a* thing. Math, computers,
music.

What kind of music?
My own, mostly.

You play an instrument?
Flute.

That was you! Was it? I heard a flute the other night.
No more. The night nurse made me stop.

It was nice.
Nice? Nice????? What kind of critical vocabulary is that?

I'm not a music critic.
But— Nice????

I wrote about your playing in my journal.
In Muktuluk, of course.

Of course.
I don't suppose you'd care to translate? You do remember what you
said

Certainly I do. Photographic memory.
So what did you say?

That your music sounded lonely. Like someone alone on a cold mountaintop.

Alien.

!! Yes. Alien.

Time to go. There's some stuff I want to do in the system, and the night watchman comes around soon. Keep using Muktuluk for anything you don't want the shrinks to see. Remember, everything that goes through the system ends up in the main memory.

So won't this little dialogue end up there, too?

Nobody'll check it out till morning, and by that time it will have vanished.

How?

Virus. What we wrote will be replaced by what looks like diary ramblings—in Muktuluk. I'll copy chunks from your other stuff. They'll never know the difference.

Can't they find viruses?

These are the people who asked a known hacker and vandal to help out in their computer lab, and you expect them to find a virus?

Doug?

Yes?

Can you get into the lab anytime you want?

Why?

Just wondered. It's lonely at midnight in the nuthouse.

Where isn't it?

Yes. Ktum.

Ktum?

Good-bye in Muktuluk. Hello is moft.

Ktum.

Ktum.

Journal—Miranda Ellenby
June 23, 2000—1:30 P.M.

Doug McAllister sat with me at lunch, so the intrusion on my screen last night really wasn't Turnbull or another shrink playing tricks.

It was a strange lunch. Tookie and Florence and Pew (watching over Timmy the Terror and another kid) sat at the same table, so we couldn't talk much. Doug used his fork and catsup to write 11 PM on a napkin. I gather this means that what we did last night he wants to do again tonight at eleven. There's a little voice inside that has spent the last half hour telling me this is a date. A "virtual" date, at least. If so, it would be the first date of any kind in my life.

Doug told Pew (when she wasn't keeping the Terror from throwing french fries) that he thought it was "nice" that the center had a computer lab. She said she supposed so but that she didn't do computers herself. I told her that computers were going to be more important to her someday than French, and she said that wouldn't be hard, since she didn't think French was ever going to do her any good, especially if she flunked it and couldn't even get the credits she needs. I said, with a perfectly straight face, that I thought French was a "nice" language. Doug laughed. He has very white teeth.

Meantime, it's a wretched day. Raining and cold and miserable, more like November than June—lake and mountains lost in gray and everybody stuck indoors. A noticeable difference in noise level with everybody inside. Can't even get away from it in the library.

The place is beginning to get to me. I thought of it as safe before, a kind of refuge from so-called civilization. But when the fog closes in I remember how cut off we are here. No outside news. Anything could be happening out there, and we wouldn't know. Creepy.

Caught Turnbull watching me this morning. I didn't like the look I saw before the smile came on. Didn't like it one bit.

FROM THE DESK OF NOAH PERIODES

To: Harlan Turnbull, M.D., Ph.D.
From: Noah Periodes, Ph.D.
Date: June 26, 2000
Re: Douglas McAllister, Patient #5043

After several sessions with Douglas McAllister, I have come to the
conclusion that our group home would be the best placement for him.

Letting him work with computers would seem to be the best way to
reach this patient. Plus, he's good. We think he'll be able to design
the best use of our equipment as well as or even better than we can,
and the challenge will keep him focused. His work with Janet in the
computer lab has shown that he has surprising skills as a teacher.
His patience with children and ability to share his own rather
impressive knowledge have been remarkable.

In addition, the group home placement will cut down on his
interaction with the other boys near his age in the lodge. So far
that interaction has proved to be entirely negative. They are either
too diminished by meds for normal socialization or antisocial in a
way that reminds him of the violence of his siblings and father, a
major source of his problems.

This is a bright young man who, if handled carefully, should be
able to deal with the problems that brought him here and take his
place again in the outside world by the time he has to leave us at
eighteen.

We would like to have him moved in by Friday, June 30th.

Journal—Miranda Ellenby
July 1, 2000—11:45 P.M.

It's 11:45, and still no Doug. He didn't contact me last night, but I just figured he must have had some kind of trouble getting into the lab. Then I didn't see him in the cafeteria today. Or anywhere else, for that matter. And it isn't as if I wasn't looking. Now I've been sitting here staring at a blank blue screen since 10:30. Nothing. What if he's gone home?

As I wrote that—What if he's gone home?—a fist balled itself up inside my stomach. The Grape is always on about how I intellectualize everything. I don't do feelings. Which is why I invented an alternate personality who "got out" in my session yesterday, one who yells and laughs and stamps her feet (the best I could do at acting feelings). This feeling right now, though, isn't acting.

I didn't cry when Mother and Daddy brought me here. I didn't cry when they drove away. Or when I found out how hard it would be to just run away. But I'm crying now. Real tears running down my cheeks—I'll probably short out my keyboard.

I'd try to reach him, but I don't want to put anything in English into the memory if Doug isn't there to plant the virus and cover it up.

We've barely even seen each other face-to-face (f2f, as he calls it). And never alone. But all day every day for a whole week, I knew I could come up here and talk to him after lights-out. Just words on the screens. And the minds behind them.

We've talked for hours, and it's as if we could keep it up forever. He hasn't explained about the wrists, and I haven't told him about Paris. It's been other things. Things neither of us has ever been able to talk about with other kids.

Me: How totally neat it is that even though there are hundreds of languages in the world, they all have some fundamental structures in common. That means they could be part of the human brain itself. Hard-wired, he calls it. And how learning language actually organizes the biology of the brain.

Him: How weird math can get, with seven-dimensional spheres, or parallel lines that converge to each other but don't touch. How patterns in music are like mathematical structures, clean and clear and elegant—"pretty," he says. How some people think music organizes the universe.

I don't scare him. And on-screen he isn't like a trapped wolf at all. He's like—I don't know, like somebody I've known all my life. Or maybe another piece of me.

That's where this all gets really weird. Last time we talked he started to tell me about this serial dream he's been having, and it's MY dream!

The whole time he was telling about it, about his gray horse and his carved wooden whistle and his feeling that he's on some kind of quest, I felt as if I'd been hit in the stomach and couldn't breathe. When I told him that we're dreaming different strands of the same dream, and about Taryn being the white cat, I said it was just too weird. Way too weird.

And he said, "The universe is a strange place. Either nothing's weird or everything is—take your pick." He thinks the dream isn't the only sign that we're connected in some way.

85

When he broke into my system that first night, he didn't really want to do it—he didn't have any idea who was online, and he could have been giving himself away. But he just couldn't help it. He felt like iron filings being pulled toward a magnet. I still get goose bumps thinking about it.

I dreamed again last night. He was in it this time, and it was dawn. Together we broke up the lean-to and scattered the ashes from the campfire, and then left—him on his gray horse, me on the black, with the white cat in front of me and the raven gliding overhead. The booming had come close enough to hear again, and we were heading away from it as fast as we could go, toward the mountains on the horizon. All day I've been dying to tell him about it. And now I can't!!!

Now here I sit at a bugged keyboard at midnight, crying like a two-year-old and writing this stupid journal for stupid posterity in stupid MUKTULUK, *a language posterity won't even understand. All alone in this stupid room with the bars on the window and the night pressing against the glass from outside.*

THIS *is why I don't do feelings!*

86

Family Ties

TARYN SAT BEHIND THE BOUNDARY of white stones at the edge of the beach, watching the ripples of clear water that moved up across the sand, pushing a fine line of white foam and tumbling bits of weed and broken shell. Behind her, she knew, Abigail sat on the porch, watching. But the watching was silent, distant. Not like at the lodge, where the only way to be outside, breathing under the open sky, had been with an aide hovering. Never able to get away from the circle of noise that surrounded and moved with every Laurel Mountain group. Never alone, never in quiet, never able to let herself slip away.

She needed that slipping away, needed to make herself part of the world of water, sky, rock, growing things. There she could soothe away her pain. In the earth's long, slow certainty there was refuge, belonging.

Taryn took a quiet breath and looked up at the mountain, where a wreath of fine cloud was wrapping itself around the peak. She reached her mind outward and up, becoming first the cloud, light and cool and fine, drifting high against gray rock, and then the mountain, massive, solid, immovable. Unconsciously, she settled herself more firmly into the grass and straightened her back. She imagined herself above the mist of encircling cloud, looking down at the world, a vast arc of woods, silvery water, fine lines of roads, and the purple-blue of distant mountains.

As she gazed out at the sweep of the land on all sides, she became aware of a thick line of shadow against the horizon. It lay threateningly at the edge of her sight, shifting against the sky. Like a living thing it seemed to pulse, rising higher here, subsiding there. Wherever she looked, the darkness was there, sucking light into itself, breathing against the sky. A deep, low rumble shook the earth beneath her.

Taryn shuddered and pulled her mind away, coming back to herself, goose bumps rising along her thin arms and across the back of her neck. She blinked and looked again, through her own eyes, from her place in the grass at the boundary stones. Sunlight. Quiet lake, reflecting the mountain's base, dimpled here and there where a fish broke the surface or a swallow dipped its beak as it swooped. Nature still untouched, unshadowed, alive.

Armageddon, her mother had called the darkness. *Not a distant prophecy*—a battle, a war already begun. Blinking again, Taryn looked at the ripples sliding up over the sand. The line of foam was pink and the water a thick bloodred.

Journal—Miranda Ellenby
July 4, 2000—11:30 P.M.

Independence Day, and I'm free of the Grape!

At breakfast Dr. Periodes—Abigail—told me about the group home, and by suppertime I was moved in. Things were crazy all day anyway—the Fourth starts summer at Laurel Mountain. They shut down morning academics and do something more like camp, with swimming and boating (for which they turn off the beach boundary alarm and bring in a battalion of lifeguards) and a nature program and arts and crafts. A big picnic kicks it off—which I missed most of.
DOUG'S HERE! And Taryn, and the little boy who

Moft. "!talkD:" gets you interactive.

!talkD: Moft! I wondered if we could do this here. When you
disappeared from the lodge I thought you'd gone home.
No such luck. Did you miss me?

It's lonely at midnight in the nuthouse, remember?
I remember.

So tell me what this group home is all about.
I don't know much yet, except that we're supposed to be a family.
If they knew *my* family they'd come up with a different term.

I know what you mean. I've never had siblings before.
You haven't missed anything!

The Periodeses are psychologists, not psychiatrists, right?
Right.

I hope that means we don't have to worry about drugs! What do
you think of them? Noah and Abigail.
They're okay. Anyway, it's better here than at the lodge.

It couldn't be much worse. This is a better computer than I
had at the lodge.
State of the art. Like everything here. The lab's fantastic. And
our system's totally separate from Turnbull's. He can't snoop.

I'll miss my view of the mountain.
You can see the lake, can't you?

A sliver through the trees.
View or not, it's better here.

I still have my ankle bracelet.
It's still a nuthouse.

From the Desk of
HARLAN TURNBULL, M.D., Ph.D.

TO: Noah and Abigail Periodes
FROM: HT
RE: Miranda Ellenby's transfer
DATE: July 4, 2000

Miranda Ellenby is *my* patient.

I'm sure you are aware that the president of the board has left for his annual Fourth of July fishing trip, so he is not available to reopen the issue of placement authority. Be assured that I intend to contact him as soon as he returns. This placement will *not* be allowed to stand!

During Miranda's stay with you, however brief, I hope you will keep in mind that she is an extremely high profile patient. Her parents could cause grave difficulties for Laurel Mountain if they should be in any way dissatisfied with their daughter's treatment. Furthermore, allowing the close contact that a group home inevitably brings between this particular patient and one whose history is as violent as Douglas McAllister's is simply irresponsible. I repeat: This placement will *not* be allowed to stand!

FROM THE DESK OF NOAH PERIODES

To: Harlan Turnbull, M.D., Ph.D.
FROM: Noah
RE: Miranda Ellenby
DATE: July 5, 2000

Please assure yourself (as we will assure Harold Deitz when he
returns) that Miranda's best interests and the best interests of the
other patients of the GFGHP's therapeutic family are our highest
priority.

A STRONG BREEZE OFF THE LAKE wafted through the living room from the broad screened windows, moving the fringe on a Hudson's Bay lap rug that hung over the railing of the loft overhead. A pair of plaid couches faced each other across a polished tree-trunk coffee table.

Noah, doodling on a legal pad, lounged at one end of one of them; Doug sat upright at the other end. Across from them Abigail and Taryn occupied the other couch, Taryn curled into herself, her feet under her. Miranda had settled into an oak rocking chair with cane back and seat, and Elijah sat cross-legged on the edge of the Indian-patterned rug, his back to the circle they made, facing the fireplace and rocking so slightly, he might have been moved only by the breeze. In one hand he turned a large clear glass marble with a blue and white swirl around and around.

"Since this is our first official family meeting, we're taping it," Noah said, gesturing at the tape recorder on the coffee table. "We'll tape them all. But the tapes won't be shared with anyone outside this room without specific permission from each of you."

Abigail pulled a partially done needlepoint pillow cover from a cloth bag at her side. "We thought you might like to know a little more about the concept of the Global Family Group Home Project, why you were chosen for it, and how it will work." She slipped on her glasses and stabbed a needle into the design, a cheetah at full run. She looked at Noah. "Background first."

"A few years ago a boy named Gordon Stephenson came to Laurel Mountain," Noah began. "The placement was pretty surprising, because he'd always been a real whiz kid. By the time he

94

was four he was playing chess, reading history, astronomy, biology, and physics. He wrote stories and poems and plays. He could do just about anything he set his mind to do."

"Except fit in with other kids," Abigail said.

"Which was the one thing he wanted most."

Miranda and Doug exchanged glances.

"It wasn't only his intelligence that set Gordon apart," Noah went on. "He was incredibly sensitive—like somebody walking around without any skin. He seemed to feel not just his own pain but everybody else's, too. He saw too much and understood it too well. His mother said that from the time he was born he seemed to be looking at the world through eyes that were a thousand years old."

"He could see that other children were happier than he was," Abigail said, "and because he couldn't know how different he was, he thought it was because they had each other. He was desperate to fit in, to make friends."

"By the time he was ten he'd decided that the reason he didn't fit was that he could do all those things other kids couldn't. So he decided to quit doing them. He persuaded his parents to send him to a new school so he could start over. Be just like everybody else." Noah paused.

Doug spoke, his voice tight. "It didn't work."

"No. He could stop doing, but he couldn't stop being. He was who he was. And who he was didn't fit. In November of that first year at the new school Gordon tried to hang himself in his bedroom closet. His mother found him in time to save his life and sent him to Laurel Mountain.

"Here, even though he was every bit as wounded as any of the other patients, he was further than ever from fitting in. He had felt himself alone for too long." Noah looked at Doug, who had leaned forward, his arms on his knees. Doug looked away.

"So what happened?" Miranda asked.

Noah looked at Abigail. "He was cured," she said.

For a moment no one said anything. "Cured?" Miranda asked finally. "How could he be cured?"

"By blocking the mind that made him vulnerable. He was given a drug that slowed everything down, interfered with his mental connections, and made him seem, to all outward appearances, normal."

"Turnbull," Miranda said. It was not a question.

"Then what?" Doug asked. "And what does this have to do with the group home?"

"We're coming to that," Noah said. "Gordon, on medication, went home. Aside from a permanent hand tremor and a kind of blankness behind his eyes, he seemed just fine. An entirely normal twelve-year-old boy."

"He could have kept from taking it," Taryn said. "They gave me pills when I first came here, and I didn't like how they made me feel. After a week I just pretended to take them. I never did again."

Abigail raised her eyebrows at Noah. "So much for the good John thought meds were doing!"

"The thing about Gordon was that he *wanted* the drugs," Noah said. "He made the choice himself. His parents moved, and he started another new school. This time he started making friends. Now, for the first time in his life, he fits. According to everyone—nearly everyone—his medication is a complete success.

He can't do the sorts of things he used to do, but he does enough to get by. They say he's still an above-average student."

Miranda and Taryn looked at each other. Doug, frowning, stared out the window toward the lake. Elijah rocked harder, spinning his marble on the floor now.

"There's suicide and there's suicide," Doug said at last.

"It was because of Gordon that we came up with the idea for the Global Family Group Home Project. If Gordon had had a place to belong, other children like himself he could share his pain with instead of denying it, he might have healed his wounds and learned to cope."

"Over the years, we'd seen other children with minds like Gordon's end up in places like Laurel Mountain. As serious as their problems are, they're caused not by what's wrong with their minds, but what's right with them. It's just that those minds are so different." Abigail poised her needle over her work. "It's like being a cheetah in a world of lions. All the things that let a cheetah run seventy miles an hour—lean body, long legs, nonretractable claws—look like deformities to the lions. Eventually, that's how it feels. Eventually, that's what many of these children become. Deformed lions."

"We decided to make a place where we could gather wounded cheetahs together," Noah said. "Let them heal. Let them know that, however few of them there are, they aren't alone. That's why the word *global* in the GFGHP. Even if there aren't many kids like this in any one place, there are lots of them in the world. If we can't bring them together in person, we can do it electronically. *And* connect them with adults who can nourish their minds and help them cope with knowing and understanding more than children are supposed to know and understand."

The silence when he had finished stopped the tape recorder.

"I suspect you can all relate to Gordon's story," Abigail said, and the low whir of the tape machine began again.

"So what you're saying"—Doug looked at Taryn and then, for a long time, at Elijah's rocking back—"is that the three of *us* are in the same league as the Baby Genius here?"

Abigail smiled. "Let's just say all four of you have extraordinary minds."

Miranda rocked back in her chair and stared at the ceiling. "Aliens," she said quietly.

Doug gestured at the log walls around them. "And this place is meant to be home planet."

Abigail nodded. "We're going to run things very differently here than up at the lodge. We genuinely mean to make this work like a family."

Doug snorted.

"A healthy family! Noah and I will be the only adults here on a regular basis. We still see patients up at the lodge, of course, so we won't both be here all the time, but one of us will be. When there are staff meetings we have to attend together, we'll have one of the aides—you'll have a vote on which one—stay with you, or you'll be able to join the activities at the lodge. Everyone will pitch in to take care of the house, and we hope, as you get comfortable with each other, you'll look after each other."

"We'll have a short meeting every weekday morning and each of you will have a daily therapy session with one of us." Noah doodled a computer screen on his pad. "In the afternoons we hope you'll hang out in our computer lab, connecting through the nets.

We've established contacts with groups doing math and chaos theory, linguistics, poetry—all the subjects we thought you might be interested in. As you start making your own contacts, you'll be free to venture in any directions you want, within reason. Besides that, we've located some 'cheetah' kids in other parts of the world. Most of them write in English, but Miranda can help with the ones who don't."

"Weekends will be weekends," Abigail added. "We'll have picnics, go for hikes, maybe eventually go camping."

Taryn stirred at the end of the couch. "We'll do everything together?"

Abigail shook her head. "Not everything. You'll each have time alone. And if you don't get enough, all you have to do is let us know." Taryn smiled and sat back again.

Noah held up his pad. He'd drawn the earth in the center of the page. "You're not aliens." He tapped the drawing with his pencil. "*This* is home planet."

Miranda rocked forward. "Great. Not aliens, just mutant freaks."

"Don't knock mutant freaks," Noah told her. "That's how evolution works. Something new appears that might turn out to be just what the species needs."

Doug shook his head. "Most mutations are just nature's screwups. Screwups that die out."

"Like Gordon Stephenson," Miranda added.

Doug looked down at his wrists. "And if they don't die out on their own, the others, the 'normals,' kill them off."

"Not always," Noah said. "And not all of them. That's the whole point, the way evolution works. *Not always.*"

"An intelligent-enough species just might do something to protect them," said Abigail. "Just might, for instance, create a Global Family Group Home."

Taryn looked from Abigail to Noah, her green eyes twinkling. "Or an ark."

Elijah stopped rocking, his marble clutched in one hand.

Noah nodded, smiling. "Or an ark."

"So," Abigail said. "Welcome to the Ark."

July 5, 2000—6:30 P.M. _____

ELIJAH PULLED HIS STRIPED BLANKET over his head and huddled in his bed, his marble clutched in one fist, the other hand wrapped around fist and marble together. Dr. Noah and later Dr. Abigail had tried to persuade him to come to dinner. But he would not.

Family, they called this. No. His family was gone.

He tried to make the white fog, to fill his head with it. But it would not come.

Last night he had had the dream again. The girl on the horse, the white cat, the boy. He had known them when they came, one at a time, to join him in this quiet house. They had disturbed the quiet, brought with them something he had no protection against. In the dream he was with them and also apart from them. As he wanted to stay. Had to stay!

He felt the hard, familiar surface of the marble and thought of the blue and white clouds that swirled together in the center. Mama Effie had given him the marble. She had told him it was like the earth. "We're all in that little ball together, child," she had told him. "All connected to each other. Looking up and out at the hand of God."

But connections didn't stay. They broke, and the people were gone. Never again would he hear the liquid sound of his mother's voice. Never again would he sit in Mama Effie's warm lap or feel her stroking away the terror of a nightmare in the darkness.

No. He did not want to be connected. Not all connections were good, anyway. Once they began you couldn't stop them, couldn't choose where the threads would lead. From his mother they had led on to the man, and the man had brought the growl, the roar.

At first when he had come to this place he had been happy to be away from the lodge, to find this stillness. He had begun to feel safe. Quiet and safe. But now he could feel the threads reaching out from himself. Threads from the others reaching in.

The night Doug had come to this place Elijah had felt tightness in his chest. It had been like the feeling from long ago when he had lain awake in the night, listening to the sirens wailing in the street, feeling his mother listening, too. Feeling her dark, dark sadness. There was such a sadness in Doug. It pulled at him, too much like his own to shut out.

And now there were the others. He did not want these connections. He did not! Tears slipped down his cheeks. He did not. And he did.

Dream-Dust

All my life
I have been a dreamer.
In the daylight I have listened to the talking of the trees
And watched hopefully, catching at times glimpses
Of unicorns in the wood.
At night my heart has wandered through meadows in
*   bloom with stars*
Along a star-filled river
And listened to them sing.
And, listening to the silence
I have heard voices
That no one else can hear.
I have heard the language of the flowers
And the poems of the brook
That sings to itself all day.
I have caught shreds of understanding
And moments in the place
Where the life of an ancient olive tree
And a mayfly
Are equally long
In a way that has nothing to do with time.
I have seen glimpses
Of the song that makes the sunset
And the hand that draws the rainbow in the sky.

Journal—Miranda Ellenby
July 5, 2000—11:35 P.M.

*Before she went to bed, Taryn brought me another poem.
"Dream-Dust." Taryn says Noah and Abigail are right about
us, but they don't know all of it.*

*Can't get the poem out of my mind. I have the oddest
feeling that it's pulling at a door in my mind that I didn't even
know was there. And now that I do know, I find that it's shut
down tight. Locked. Barred. How to get it open? Do I want to?*

*The talking of the trees, the singing of stars. Have I ever
heard what Taryn hears? So long ago that it's gone, like the
sights and sounds of being born?*

"All my life...a dreamer."

*Images are beginning to come, like scenes from an old
movie. But nothing as mystical as unicorns and singing stars.
Not dreams. Memories.*

*There's a television screen filled with faces crying, the sound
of screams. A war somewhere. A little girl with empty eyes, her
dress torn, her face streaked with dirt or blood, sitting on a pile
of broken stones. I can see into those eyes, feel her terror, her
grief and pain. FEEL THEM! Then I am climbing the blue-
carpeted stairs, my vision blurred with tears, hurrying down the
hall to my bedroom. I can't be more than two. I can see my
bear Tulu through the bars of my crib as I go past.*

*I'm stretching up for my piggy bank, then carrying it, one
step at a time, down the stairs and into the living room. I'm
telling Mother and Daddy they should send the money in it to*

103

the little girl whose house has been bombed. I'm crying so hard I can hardly talk.

Then Mother leans down, face and hands huge, and takes the bank. She tells me everything is going to be all right, that nobody will bomb our house.

As if I am afraid for MYSELF!

As I wrote that, another memory came. This one a dream. No. A nightmare. How could I have forgotten?

It went on night after night. Maybe year after year. A coincidence, Abigail talking about lions and cheetahs. A purple lion—purple!—chasing me to the basement of the house, cornering me there, all by myself in the darkness.

That night—that night with the piggy bank—was the first night.

This isn't just memory coming up. This isn't as simple as that. My hands are shaking at the keyboard as I write. It isn't only the lion, teeth and claws and destruction. It's having to face it all by myself.

That's what Mother wanted me to be, what everyone wanted me to be. Separate. An "I" whose house wasn't bombed when another child's was, who didn't need to cry when someone else felt pain. And eventually didn't need to cry at all. I was a good little girl, a smart little girl. Smart, smart, smart. The smartest little girl in all the world. I did what they wanted me to do.

And met the purple lion in the night.

DOUG, AT THE TERMINAL IN HIS room, signed off and pushed back his chair. The networking would be good. Once he got comfortable with the terminology, the chaos conference was going to be terrific. And the math conference felt like coming home. It was better than anything, even the Advanced Placement stuff he'd had in school. But the rest of it...

Noah wanted him to teach Elijah and Taryn. How was he supposed to teach a kid who wouldn't even look at him?

Global family. Miranda as his sister. Not exactly the relationship he had in mind.

Doug looked at the puckery pinkish purple skin of the scars on his wrists. Like twin zippers. They would flatten out eventually, he knew. And turn white. But they would always be there.

He was no Gordon Stephenson, feeling the pain of a world he understood too well. Doug understood the world, all right. It was a place where guns won out over knives and knives over tire irons and tire irons over fists and fists over minds. You could accept that and find a place there, or you could let it roll over you, take you out. Noah had asked him what he'd been feeling the night he'd done it. He'd had the answer, but it wasn't pain. *Rage.*

Rage had not vanished with the shattering of glass. It had worn itself out, maybe. Fallen back for now. But it was like the puckered lines across his wrist—once there, always there.

The ark idea was no good. It wasn't the thought that they were mutations that bothered him. He'd thought that himself. The problem was that it wouldn't work. You could coddle mutations

105

for a while, but while you were protecting them, the outside world would be going on the way it always had. They couldn't ride out the flood in this ark, because the flood would never go down. Whenever they got out of here their mutation would trigger the same old response. Same response, same result. And if they couldn't fight back, didn't have whatever that fight took, they'd be gone. Extinct. Kaput.

Survival of the fittest was how the regular world worked. And Doug knew who the fittest were, no question—the ones who saw the world their own way and could make it work for them. The ones who could say to hell with people who got in their way. Not just people. Anything—animals, plants, oceans. Music. The fittest were the ones who didn't care.

No matter how safe they might be here in this "family," no matter how many friends they made with other kids around the world, or how connected they got to each other, there weren't enough of them. And when they went out into the world, the fittest would be waiting for them.

He'd had the dream again last night. They'd been riding toward the mountains, the guns booming behind them, closer and closer. He had touched the wooden whistle at his waist and wished instead for a bow and arrow, a sword, a spear. And then, as the raven swooped and landed on his shoulder, its claws sharp through his cloak, he had smiled, remembering his ax.

Doug picked up the flute that lay next to his keyboard and turned it over in his hands. He put it to his lips and blew gently. One note. Another. And then his fingers, his lips, his breath took over and the music spilled into the room, bringing, as it always did, a pure, clean light.

Journal—Miranda Ellenby
July 10, 2000—1:15 A.M.

So far the GFGHP's a bust! Taryn will hardly set foot in the lab. The cousins she lived with before she got sent here did nothing with their computers except play blood-and-guts games. She can't seem to get over the idea that computers are somehow the enemy. She stays outdoors whenever she can, and when she's inside she's always looking out, the way she used to do at the lodge. Maybe that's part of why she avoids the lab—it doesn't have any windows.

And Elijah! He goes to the lab in the afternoon, but then he just sits and rocks in front of his terminal. Doug explains the networks and demonstrates how to do things, but Elijah won't make any effort to do any of them. What good is an extraordinary mind, assuming he really has one, if he keeps it locked inside that small, rocking body?

The monitors in the lab spend more time swirling the colored fractals of their screen savers than making global family connections.

July 10, 2000—2:30 P.M. _____

MIRANDA, TIRED OF LISTENING TO Doug trying to persuade Elijah to type something on his keyboard, had suggested they all take a break from the computer lab. "Doug could play his flute for us," she had told Noah, ignoring the look Doug gave her over the top of his monitor. And so they had gathered in the living room. She

107

and Taryn sat now on one couch, Noah and Abigail on the other. Elijah was in his usual spot in front of the fireplace, spinning his marble on the hearth.

Doug, perched gingerly on the arm of Noah and Abigail's couch, turned his flute around and around in his hands. "Don't expect too much," he said. "This piece isn't really finished yet."

"We're very forgiving," Noah said, leaning back and closing his eyes. "Besides, you're the best flute player we have. Go to it."

"Okay." Doug took a long, slow breath, put his flute to his lips, and began to play.

The silvery notes wove themselves through the room's stillness, and Taryn sighed, snuggling back against the cushions. Like a cat getting comfortable, Miranda thought. When she was still again, one bare foot rested lightly against Miranda's leg. As they listened, the point of contact between them began to feel warm.

Suddenly, Miranda had the sensation that she was experiencing the music not only with her ears but also through that spot of warmth, as if the sound were moving through Taryn to her and back again, a thread weaving them to each other and to Doug as he played. She closed her eyes and rested her cheek against her arm on the back of the couch. The music rippled like water around her.

Images formed in Miranda's mind one after another—the mountain across the lake reflected in a still, mirrored surface; stars coming out against a darkening sky; and then the northern lights, wavering across the darkness in ghostly banners of pink and green. Sound and touch and vision ran together until she could not tell where one sensation ended and another began. Transported to another realm, she knew only that the others were there with her, and she wanted to stay.

When Doug finished Miranda didn't move. She seemed to have to pull herself back into her body, into the room, into the silence. Finally, Abigail spoke. "That was lovely, Doug."

Noah cleared his throat loudly. Miranda opened her eyes and followed his gaze to Elijah, who had shifted his position. He was leaning now against Doug's blue jean–clad leg, his body still, his marble in one hand.

"Glad you liked it." Doug lowered his flute and rested a hand lightly on Elijah's shoulder. Elijah didn't move.

"Have you ever seen the northern lights?" Miranda asked Doug.

He looked at her, his eyes wide. "That's what I call this piece! 'Northern Lights.'"

"There were stars in it, too," Taryn said. "First there were stars."

Doug nodded.

"And the mountain and the lake," Taryn added.

In the long silence, Noah and Abigail exchanged a look.

"Does anyone else play an instrument?" Abigail asked. "We might work up a little group. I could dig out my old guitar."

Noah chuckled. "Beware. I'll get out my kazoo."

Miranda, wishing now that she had studied music, and could make such magic, shook her head. "I never had time to learn."

"Taryn?" Abigail asked.

Taryn didn't answer. She was staring out the front window, her gaze seemingly anchored by something far away. There was nothing dreamy about her look, though, Miranda thought. Her whole body seemed to be tuned like a harp string, all but vibrating with concentration. She held up a hand then, as if to keep everyone silent. Miranda found herself holding her breath.

Suddenly, from in front of the house, there came a long, sharp birdcall, eerily textured, as if two notes were being sung at once. It was followed by a trill and a series of notes with that same internal harmony; then the whole thing was repeated. After a moment, the series was repeated again, closer. And then a speckle-breasted brown bird a little smaller than a robin appeared at the front window, perched on the wide sill. It sang again, that single ethereal note followed by the trill of three, repeated at a slightly higher pitch. Once more it sang, and then, with a flash of rusty tail, the bird was gone, and the only sound from outdoors was a breeze in the trees overhead.

Taryn did that, Miranda thought to herself. She called that bird. Doug, his hand still on Elijah's shoulder, caught her eye. She did that, Miranda thought again, and Doug nodded, as if he'd heard.

July 10, 2000—11:45 P.M. _____

It was a hermit thrush she called. I looked it up.
Remember what I said—either nothing's weird or everything is.
Everything, then. And what did you do with that flute of yours?
Elijah leaned against your leg. Let you touch him!
Music hath charms. :-)
I'm not kidding. Something happened when you played. Like
nothing I ever felt before.
I know. Did you see what Elijah did in the lab afterward? He got

110

himself out on the nets. He must have been listening all along—
remembering, too.

So, maybe they're right. Maybe the global family thing—the
Ark—will work after all.

Save the mutants? Nice dream, but no way.

Why not?

Think about what it's like out there, Miranda. The UN published a
report a while back—you must have heard about it. It said the
world's worse today than it's ever been. Ethnic violence and
warfare. Massacres and murders. Crime. Domestic violence. Even child
abuse. They're growing at a rate no one's ever seen before. Not
just because the population's growing—more in proportion to the
number of people. There was the Holocaust in the '40s, Cambodia in
the '70s, Eastern Europe in the '90s. But this isn't just happening
in one place. It's everywhere, all at once. The report called it a
pandemic of violence. Homo sapiens's self-invented plague.

Homo sapiens. Intelligent man.

Just remember who named us that! You, of all people, should know
better. How smart do you feel?

Comparatively?

No. Just you yourself. How smart do you really feel?

Truth?

Of course, truth!

I've spent my whole life trying not to know how scary it was to
have people call me the smartest kid in the world. Because I
don't know anything.

So what does that tell you about everybody else? Homo sapiens? Homo
horribilis is more like it. Look what we've made with what brain we
have—guns and bombs and gas chambers.

That's not all we've made. A human brain thought up your flute!

Besides, we can change. We have enough brain to change!

How? Morality? Ethics? Religion? We've had all of recorded history for those to work, and look where we are. Violence is bred in the bone. Think about it. Suppose you and I disagree—big-time. If I won't kill you but you're perfectly willing to kill me, who wins? You do. The killer. Every time.

What about Gandhi? What about Martin Luther King?

Gunned down. Both of them, gunned down. Violence wins, Miranda. If you can't fight back, if you can't fight harder, you lose. See? It doesn't matter whether we fit anywhere or not. The UN report's world is the world we have to go out and live in. Us with our puny little brains. Me with my flute. We haven't got a chance.

Yeah? Well, maybe we do. Something happened today when you played that flute. And Taryn called a hermit thrush to sing for us!

July 13, 2000—1:45 P.M. _____

DOUG SENT HIS MESSAGE AND then leaned back in his chair, rolling his head around to loosen the tight muscles across his shoulders. He had helped Janet in the lab at the lodge in the morning instead of swimming with the others and had spent too much time at the screen today. But he couldn't help it. In spite of what he'd told Miranda the other night, he'd been hooked. He stretched his legs. The hike Noah had proposed for after dinner would have to make up for all this sitting.

Hooked. Not by the nets. There was nothing different about those. What was different had to do with Elijah. With what had

112

started happening the afternoon he'd played his flute. Like stones dropping out of a wall, a hole opening, a small hand reaching through. And it wasn't only Elijah. Taryn, too. And Miranda. Something he couldn't explain. If the Ark *could* work, it had to. No matter what happened afterward. And that depended on the connections he was making now, the connections he was trying to make.

Today had been especially successful. When he'd logged on there had been a message waiting for him from Akeylah, an eleven-year-old girl whose father was a professor at Wayne State in Detroit. He'd gotten four names of math prodigies from the people on the math conference, and Akeylah was the only girl. So he'd contacted her to see if she wanted a net pal. Even though her specialty was math, he'd been hoping there would be something about her that would interest Taryn, help persuade her to try making connections this way. He knew, even though he couldn't explain it, how important it was. "Computers are no worse than phones," he'd told her. "You wouldn't mind talking to Miranda on the phone, would you? The point is two people communicating, not the technology they use."

Taryn had not been impressed. Not yet. After all, if she wanted to talk to Miranda or any of them, all she had to do was talk. And she didn't seem to need or even want anyone else. What he needed to do was find someone far away that Taryn would want to talk to enough to risk the technology.

Akeylah's answer to his first message had been perfect. Math turned out to be her secondary interest. What she liked most were animals. She wanted to be a field biologist, wanted to save endangered species. Right age, right interests. And she was eager to connect with other kids. Better yet, though most of her network connections were with math people, she was already interacting with a girl in Lithuania whose passion was not only animals but plants, too. Maybe he could persuade Taryn to send these two girls one of her poems. He tapped a key to print out Akeylah's message. Hard copy might be the way to hook Taryn.

He stood up, stretched, and went around the bank of computers to where two printers were spitting pages into their trays. Miranda stood at one, gathering pages.

Miranda looked over at Elijah, who sat at the last computer in the row, hunched over the keyboard, tapping steadily. "He's incredible, isn't he?" she whispered. "I've never seen anybody pick anything up so fast in all my life."

Doug nodded. "No need to whisper. His mind's like a laser beam. When he's concentrating you have to touch him to get his attention. The day after he first put his fingers on the keys he was touch-typing. Now he makes me look slow! And he never forgets a thing. If I've said it, he knows it. He may not talk face-to-face, but he's been communicating with some kids Noah and Abigail found before we started this—a boy in Jerusalem, a girl in Spain."

"What's he doing now?"

"I don't know. He stuck with e-mail for a while, but he's surfing now. I started him looking for weather maps."

"Too bad we can't get Taryn doing this," Miranda said. "I told her about the poetry section on Kidweb, but she wasn't interested. Guess she wouldn't find much kid poetry she could relate to."

Doug shook his head. "Where is she?"

"Outside, as usual. Abigail gave up watching her every second and set some boundaries. As long as she stays inside them, she can go out on her own. I think I know what she's doing out there."

"What?"

"Same thing we are. Networking."

"With birds?" Doug picked up the printout of Akeylah's message.

"Birds. Trees. The mountain, maybe."

July 13, 2000—2:17 P.M. _____

TARYN SAT CROSS-LEGGED AT the base of a tree, watching an ant crawl across her knee. It was carrying a bit of something—she couldn't tell what—half as big as itself. She wondered if it minded the burden, the effort it was making. Then she wondered if it thought she was a permanent obstacle, like a mountain, in its way, wherever it was going. If it thought there was no way around her, so it had to struggle over, up her leg, across her knee, down again. Maybe it didn't think at all, just sensed the huge presence of her sitting self and began the climb. She took a breath and sent her mind toward it as it made its way down her shin.

After a moment, she shook her head. It was no good. Imagining her way into an ant was like imagining her way into an eyelash, a fingernail, a blood cell. The ant didn't feel whole. It didn't feel like a separate creature at all. If she wanted to know how it was to be an ant, maybe she needed to reach into its colony. Maybe the colony was a whole creature, not this single worker that had crossed to the other shin now and was doggedly moving up toward the other knee. And the colony's mind? Where was that?

Was it in the queen? Or was it just somehow made up of all of them, in the togetherness of the way they worked, in the messages they sent among themselves?

Taryn held her finger in front of the ant. It went around. Twice more she tried to get it to come onto her hand so she could put it on the ground. Finally, she brushed it gently off onto the grass, where it went on, struggling now along a grass blade, as if nothing had happened.

She sighed and leaned against the tree. She closed her eyes, feeling the steadiness of it against her back, the long, slow, quiet life of a rooted thing. A woodpecker drummed somewhere nearby, the sound seeming to echo hollowly among the trees.

Taryn felt a sudden searing pain, like a knife slashing at her stomach. She opened her eyes. Blood covered her legs, pooled at her feet. She raised her hands, as if to ward off a blow, and saw them, too, drenched in blood. She gasped. Blinked. And the pain, the blood—both vanished as quickly as they had come, leaving her shivering in the dappled sunlight beneath the tree. Before she could sort it out, think what had happened, a sound seemed to pierce her brain—a high, thin keening.

Elijah. And she was up and running toward the house.

July 13, 2000—2:24 P.M. _____

"WHAT HAPPENED?" NOAH, OUT OF breath from his plunge downstairs, stood at the door of the computer lab.

116

"We don't know," Doug said. "Scared us to death. He just started making that sound and then he bolted. Like he couldn't get out of here fast enough."

"He headed for his room," Miranda said.

Noah rubbed at his beard. "Just when things seemed to be going so well for him. I'll go see—"

"Taryn's with him," Miranda interrupted. "She was here almost before he got out the door. When she went into his room he stopped yelling at least."

Doug looked up from Elijah's computer screen. "Look here." The others moved to look over Doug's shoulder. "He'd been surfing the nets. He must have stumbled on a news service."

```
Path:
Laurel.grt.com!netnews.upenn.edu!crabapple.srv.cs.smu.edu!looking!
bass!clarinews
From: clarinews@clarinet.com (Reuters)
Distribution: clari.apo
Message-ID: <mtunda-murtuURb74_4oN@clarinet.com>
Date:Thurs, 13 Jul 00 9:20:50PDT


> MTUNDA (Reuters)—Tigal tribe members have massacred all the
> inhabitants of three villages in the latest outbreak of tribal
> fighting in this tiny mountainous country. The bodies of thousands
> of men, women, and children of the Murtu tribe have been found by
> UN relief workers who braved sporadic Tigal attacks to get through
> to the isolated villages. They had hoped to bring food and medical
> relief but found to their horror that there were no survivors.
>     "In two decades of disaster relief work I've never seen anything
```

> like this," one member of the UN team said. "Most of these people
> were slashed with machetes or bludgeoned to death. Children,
> babies, pregnant women. I can't talk any more about it."
>   It is not clear what set off this most recent action. But the
> level of violence, always high between the two tribes, is
> escalating.
>   Reached in Geneva, where he is vacationing, UN Secretary General
> Khana said, "It is not the violence itself that is new, merely its
> scope and intensity. Once one could speak of hot spots. Now the
> world itself is hot."

July 13, 2000—3:30 P.M. _____

TARYN TURNED THE SWIVEL CHAIR she was sitting in away from the
computer. "My mother called it Armageddon."

"Armageddon?" Doug said. "That's the war at the end of the
world. The biblical prophecy."

Taryn's eyes flashed. "It isn't a prophecy anymore. It's happening! Darkness against light. My mother said people expect
Armageddon to be a world war, one side against the other. Bad
guys and good guys. But it isn't. It's all of it—crime and riots and
terrorism and massacres like that one." She gestured at the printout of the story Elijah had found.

"If your mother was right, there's nothing we can do about
it." Doug stared at the fist he had made in his lap. He opened it
slowly and closed it again. "We might as well all hide under a desk
like Elijah."

"No!" Taryn said. "We can't let it shut us down. That's what

I told Elijah. We can't do what he's been doing, close up like clams and push it all away. Because we're meant for something. Hurting so much when we see what's happening out there—caring so much—that's meant for something, too."

"Yeah," Doug said, "it's meant to push Gordon Stephenson to take Turnbull's way out. Why not, if it's the end of the world?"

Taryn shook her head. "It would be the end only if darkness won! Shutting down, no matter how we do it, helps the darkness."

"How do we keep from shutting down," Miranda asked, "when it hurts so much?"

"By making connections," Taryn said.

Doug waved his hands at the computers. "You won't even try."

"Not that way."

"How?" Miranda asked.

"It's like Noah and Abigail said. It helps not to be alone with it. To share it. But not just with other kids. We can connect with everything else—the mountain, the lake, the woods."

Doug frowned. "*You* can, you mean."

"*We* can," Taryn said.

"You're telling me I can have a conversation with a mountain?"

"Not a conversation exactly. You must have done it before, growing up here. Didn't you feel different—calmer—when you were out in the woods by yourself? In a canoe? Watching the northern lights?"

Doug started to shake his head and then stopped, his brow furrowed.

"Those were connections," Taryn said. "I can teach you how to make them on purpose, make them stronger. It's important. A mountain doesn't feel the way we do about things—"

"A mountain doesn't feel at all!"

Taryn sighed. "If you connect with something that's been around, hardly changing at all, for millions and millions of years, you get a different sense of what's important."

"All right. But we have to do more than survive. What are we supposed to do? If this is Armageddon, what's our part in it?"

"I don't know," Taryn said.

Doug gestured at the monitors with their glowing, ever-moving screen savers. "Whatever it is, whatever we're for, you can bet the four of us aren't enough. There's a heck of a lot of brain power out there that isn't in this house right now. The rest of the mutant freaks. I gather you told Elijah he can't just run away anymore. Or shut himself up the way he does. You told him about connecting to mountains?"

"Yes."

"So essentially you told him that he has to change his coping strategy, the way he's been handling his pain. He has to find a new way to survive."

"That's Noah and Abigail's message," Miranda said. "Every group meeting. Every private session, too, at least for me. 'Whatever you did to get yourself this far, it isn't working anymore.'"

"Right. We're all of us in a nuthouse with electronic shackles on our ankles because our survival strategies weren't working. It seems to me Elijah's already changed his strategy. More than any of us! He's come out of his shell and made contact with other kids on his computer. The same computer that brought that nasty little bit of 'Armageddon' in here. So what about you, Taryn?"

"Me?"

"Are you going to change? You sit outside talking to mountains. When are you going to start using these computers and connecting to people? If your kind of connecting is important, so is the one Noah and Abigail set up here." Doug dug a folded piece of paper out of his back pocket and handed it to Taryn. "I'll make you a bargain. I'll take lessons in connecting with mountains from you if you'll let me show you how to connect with Akeylah in Detroit. And Violeta, her net pal in Lithuania."

Taryn held the paper for a moment. Then she unfolded it and read the words. She read it again, running a finger over the printing, and then looked up. She nodded. "When do we start?"

July 15, 2000—4:30 A.M._____

MIRANDA SAT UP, BLINKING IN the dim light of her room. "Dream," she whispered to herself, reassured to hear her own voice, glad that dawn light was coming into the world outside to push back the darkness. "Only a dream, a nightmare."

A huge shadowed figure had loomed in front of her, back turned, fists raised like hammers about to smash something, someone, to pieces. Past him, huddled against something flat and white—a refrigerator door—crouched a thin woman, eyes squeezed shut in a dark mahogany face.

Get away, Mama! Run! Now! Through a roar that filled her head like a tornado, overriding all sound, Miranda formed the

121

words, flinging them outward as hard as she could from her place on the floor, words without speech, without sound. But the fists had thundered down, and a scream broke through the roar, shattering her sleep.

Miranda sat very still, searching the dream for something familiar. Nothing. She had been herself and someone else. It was like someone else's dream, someone else's memory. She ran it again in her head, reliving each image. The roar in her head a warning of the man's violence, a warning she had not been able to make the woman feel. When the blows descended, she had tucked herself into a tight ball on the cold tiles of a gritty floor. Then she remembered. Something familiar. The feel of a marble, hard and round, in her fist.

LAUREL MOUNTAIN CENTER FOR RESEARCH AND REHABILITATION

FAX: PAGE 1 OF 1
TO: Harold Deitz, President of the Board
FROM: HT
DATE: July 17, 2000
RE: Placement authority for GFGHP

Welcome back. I hope the fishing was good.

Sorry to greet your return with trouble, but we have a situation that in my opinion endangers a patient and perhaps Laurel Mountain itself.

In your absence, the Periodeses chose Miranda Ellenby as the fourth member of their "family." Miranda Ellenby is my patient, and I do not believe that a group home placement with its intense interaction is appropriate for a fragile and fragmented personality such as hers. Furthermore, one of the other "family" members is a violent and unstable teenaged boy. The implications are obvious.

As you know, I cannot monitor the day-to-day operations of the project because the plan allows the Periodeses to keep staff (including myself) at a distance.

Miranda Ellenby and her parents are known around the world. Any misstep on our part could result in disastrous publicity and an almost-certain lawsuit.

I believe that the board should review the issue of placement authority immediately. This is precisely the sort of problem I feared when I objected to being cut out of the decision-making process in the first place. I'm sure the board, whatever its business acumen and philosophical enthusiasm for our mission, does not wish to put itself in the position of overriding the medical director's authority on medical matters.

P.O. BOX 1295 LAUREL RIDGE, NEW YORK 12929 (518) 555-4500

DEITZ REALTY

322 Lakeview Dr., Lake Placid, NY 12108 (518) 555-3322

```
To:      Harlan Turnbull
From:    Harold Deitz, President of the Board
Date:    July 17, 2000
Re:      Your FAX of 7/17—GFGHP
```

As you know, I have considerable faith in both the Periodeses and their project. I think we can safely assume they're aware of the publicity implications of Miranda Ellenby's case and are guarding her welfare with their usual fervor.

Let's ride with this for a while, Harlan. As you pointed out, the board dislikes making decisions related to patient care. They prefer to leave medical matters in the hands of the professional staff. The approval of this project had built into it from the start a reliance on two members of that staff whose work has been impeccable over the years. It is simply too soon to begin second-guessing the original decision. Furthermore, a change now would require an emergency meeting, and it would be difficult to gather even the executive committee during this prime vacation time.

Next time I'm there, we might just drop in on the project together. That will give you a chance to allay your fears and me a chance to see that incredibly expensive computer lab in operation.

The fishing was great!

Journal—Miranda Ellenby
July 19, 2000—11:50 P.M.

*Head and heart. Abigail says I've never had any balance
between those two. That isn't all that much different from what
Turnbull said about being a hermit in my mind, but it sure feels
different. This isn't about being* NORMAL, *it's about being sane.
Healthy. Okay.*

*When you aren't normal, you don't know how normal
people think (except that it's different from how you think), so
you don't know how they feel, either. You can't connect with
them. You can't* DO *heart.*

*What if heads are different from person to person but hearts
aren't?*

*Maybe fear is just fear. And pain is pain. What makes
people afraid may not be the same, but the way afraid feels is.
Before that dream the other night, I looked at Elijah from the
outside. I saw a crazy little kid at first, and then I saw a
super-brilliant computer prodigy crazy little kid. And now
suddenly there's somebody different there. Because that dream
was Elijah's memory. Now there's a terrified little boy who's in
a whole lot of pain. In that dream his fear felt exactly like mine
when the lion was chasing me, only his was no nightmare. His
was real.*

*I must have known about feelings when I was two. So I'm
not learning this, I'm just finding it again.*

*On the other hand, I've been trying to learn Taryn's
"connecting" for three whole days, and for the first time in my
life there's something I can't learn. It's so easy for Taryn that it's*

hard for her even to tell us how to start, and I can't figure it out! We all sat on a blanket on the grass, looking up at Laurel Mountain on Monday afternoon after morning camp was over and things were quiet, while Taryn tried to teach us how to connect. "Reach," is what she said first. "Get relaxed, look at the mountain, and reach with your mind until you get inside it."

Right. I can do a lot with my mind, but I don't have any idea how to REACH *with it. I tried thinking about what the mountain is made of. How old it is. How big it is. No good. The thing is, I need to understand this process to do it. I need to know how it works.*

Elijah didn't have any such problem. He sat there, cross-legged as always (like a skinny Buddha), and sort of went away. No rocking, no sound—you could hardly tell he was breathing. It was almost like watching him turn into a mountain right there in front of us. He was so into it that when Abigail called us to help fix dinner, Doug had to shake him to bring him out of it.

I told myself I lost my concentration when I noticed that Turnbull had come out of the lodge and was watching us. Watching me. It wasn't the first time I'd noticed him lurking, and it gives me a creepy feeling. But that's just an excuse, probably. I hate it that there's something I can't do with my mind! I'd have felt worse about not being able to do it, except that Doug couldn't do it either.

It's working for Elijah, just like Taryn said it would. The next day when he pulled in a terrible news story about the bombing of a soccer stadium in France, he didn't run. He started to make that sound again, that awful grating, keening sound, and Taryn told him to connect. Almost instantly he stopped moaning. Next thing we knew, he was cross-legged in his chair, being a mountain again.

*More than two hundred people died in that bombing, and thousands were hurt. There was a color photo with it—I couldn't look. It was the terrorist group that the soldiers were trying to guard against when I was in Paris that did it. All those ordinary people just going to a soccer game. One man lost both legs and an arm—just going to a soccer game! I kept thinking about what Taryn said—*ARMAGEDDON.

Today Taryn tried to teach Doug and me by using a computer-generated 3-D poster, one of those things called a stereogram that looks like just a really intricate design until you look at it right and see the three-dimensional image "inside" it. Noah uses it with patients to talk about learning to look at your problems in a different way. Taryn said you don't have to understand how the poster works (though Doug does, naturally!) to see the 3-D image. You just have to see it with your mind instead of your eyes.

She says the world is like that poster. There's a surface— the trees and mountains and lakes and animals and people and buildings—everything we think of as real—the world. And then there's another world sort of behind it. It's every bit as real, only you can't touch it. You can only sense it, sort of like seeing and hearing it, but not exactly. Like her poem about hearing the stars sing. You see and hear it with your mind's eyes and ears instead of your body's.

Doug and I were both trying too hard, she said. Like people

127

focusing harder and harder on the poster's surface design.
Trying to force their eyes to see. "Maybe I shouldn't have told
you to REACH. *To see the image in the poster you have to*
relax—let your eyes go out of focus until you get the sense that
something is moving, slipping backward, and then you see it."

Well, that I can do. No problem. And I know that the more
you do it, the easier it gets. Taryn says that's true about
connecting, too. Except that I can't do that even the first time.
She says you have to relax. Quit thinking about it. You have to
"not try." How do you NOT *try?*

Moft. Are you there?

>   *!talkD: Moft yourself. It's after midnight. What're you doing up?*
I did it!

>   *Did what?*
Connected.

>   *Are you telling me I'm the only one who can't do it now?*
:-) But you can! I was sitting here in my room, staring out at the
tree by my window, trying to connect. Getting nowhere as usual.
Then I got the idea to pretend I was the tree. The way a little kid
would. I imagined bark all over me, and roots reaching down into
the ground. I imagined what it would be like to have to stay in one
place no matter what happened. Rain, wind—fire. Not being able to
run if there was a fire. And all of a sudden, I felt it. Like I
was the tree! It's hard to explain. Needles and wind and insects
and a sort of quiet feeling because of the dark. Not sleep, just
stillness. It was just as if the tree was letting me know how it
felt. Telling me in some way. It was amazing!

>   *The word for that isn't connecting. It's imagination!*

128

How do we know imagination isn't just a different way of knowing something? A message from outside.

It was a message from your own brain, figuring out how a tree ought to feel. That's what imagination is. No magic, just your brain. Chemistry and electrical impulses.

First I was using what I know about trees, like you said. And then the rest of it was just there, as if it was coming from the tree. It didn't take any effort at all. I'm telling you, I connected!

You're just trying to show up the Baby Genius.

And you're just jealous because I did it first. I'm telling you, just try it. *Try it!* I'm signing off now so you can. Ktum.

Okay, okay. Ktum.

If he can, I can!

July 22, 2000

TARYN WATCHED THE WIND ERASE the mountain's reflection in the water, sunlight touching the ripples with glitters of gold. The Ark family had hiked to the opposite end of the lake from the lodge and were gathered now on a spit of land between the main body of the lake and the reedy shallows. Smoke from their campfire rose, coiling above the flames, and then spread like a tattered banner into the treetops.

Noah and Abigail were preparing dinner. Elijah sat near the fire, holding his marble up to its light. Doug and Miranda had begun skipping stones across the sheltered crescent of still water close to shore. Family.

129

Taryn looked up at the mountain and sighed. The line of darkness she had seen that day before Miranda came to the Ark, the darkness looming on the horizon, was growing. Coming closer. She could feel it behind every connection, as if the earth itself sensed its power. There was strength in the family's coming together, learning to reach. But there was strength in the darkness, too.

She looked down now as Doug and Miranda moved closer to where she sat.

"Bet you can't beat six," Doug was saying.

"Eight!" Miranda said, picking up another stone. "This one's good for eight."

"Nine!" Taryn called.

Miranda turned to her and their eyes locked. Taryn smiled, making a picture of it in her mind. Miranda grinned. "Okay, sure—what the heck. Nine!"

Taryn concentrated on the picture, a stone skipping across water, clearly enough to count the splashes as it went—six, seven, eight...nine.

Miranda blinked. She gave her head a little shake, then turned back toward the water. "Here goes!" She weighed the stone a moment in her hand, glanced over her shoulder at Taryn, and then, with a sharp flip of the wrist, sent it skimming across the surface of the water. Like a flying saucer sampling the water, the stone touched and rose, touched and rose, touched and rose, leaving a trail of droplets behind it. Eight times it touched the surface before it vanished on the ninth, the ripples it had left behind crisscrossing and intermingling in a confusion of reflected light.

"Nine!" Miranda shouted. "Ha!" Her voice held triumph. And awe.

Doug looked from one to the other. "Why don't I find that surprising?"

"It's all in the wrist," Miranda said. "Isn't it?"

Taryn nodded.

"I've got this terrific wrist."

"Sure." Doug ran his hand through his lengthening brush cut. "I think Noah could probably use some help with the hamburgers," he said. Taryn watched him go, watched him pat Elijah's head as he passed, watched Elijah turn to look after him. Then she met Miranda's gaze.

"I don't think I even want to ask," Miranda said. She walked away along the shore, her eyes on the ground, as if looking for skipping stones.

Taryn rested her chin on her knees and let her mind go quiet. A pair of loons well out on the water caught her attention. She took a long, slow breath and let herself feel the dark water as they ducked their heads and sliced cleanly down. The sunlight, the smell of the campfire, the sound of tiny waves rippling against the shore, and the voices of Doug and Noah faded into cool darkness. She felt the sleek and certain plunge toward the movement of a silvery swirl of fish.

Suddenly, layering itself over the sensations, the images in her mind, came a smell—the heavy, sweet smell of blood. Behind her, Doug had reached for the hamburger, torn the plastic wrap. He stood now looking down, blood leaking between his fingers.

The smell grew stronger. Taryn swallowed, tightening the grip of her arms around her knees as she felt herself slip away. She was kneeling in a dim and snowy clearing between encircling trees, the darkness of firs and the white of birch. Before her in the dawning light lay the body of a deer—a doe, eyes glazed in death, mouth open beneath a soft black nose. Blood stained the snow beneath the animal's chest.

Taryn shivered, chilled through, fingers and toes numb with cold. Hunger gnawed at her, and she heard a voice, the memory of a voice. As surely as she heard, she understood. A father's voice, cold as the snow. "Ten years old—past time to grow up. We'll be back at eight tomorrow. If it isn't done, you don't come home. Understand that, boy—you don't come home."

She looked down and watched a hand, stiff in its dark glove, hold up a hunting knife. She remembered the long, frightened, sleepless night, huddled beneath fir boughs, arms inside the down jacket, breathing into a scarf wrapped tightly to catch warm breath and hold it in. *Won't*—that had been the thought, through the long darkness. *I won't!* But hunger was winning, as the implacable voice had known it would. Hunger and cold.

Taryn watched as the hands at last moved knife against fur. She felt herself pressing with all her strength, felt the sharp blade cut through fur and skin into the dark red beneath. It sawed raggedly into muscle and sinew. The smell of blood and cold flesh rose in the chill air. Hands and knife were not enough against bone. Taryn, sickness burning in her throat, felt herself struggle to her feet, wedge a stone beneath the nearly severed head and stomp on the neck, listening for the crack of vertebrae.

When at last it was done, the head lying in a hollow in the trampled, bloody snow, Taryn threw down the knife. A swipe of gloves across her face mingled tears and blood. A new cold was rising inside. *Dad won,* the thought came. *He always will.*

The headless carcass would get home, strapped for the world

to see across the old truck's fender, with no head to show it an out-of-season doe. *Now I am part of this. One of them. A member of the family.* Still the cold rose inside, freezing the memory of what had been lost.

"Hamburgers are on! Come get your beans and chips."

Noah's voice shattered the vision, and Taryn blinked in the sudden warmth of the early-evening sunlight. Doug was crouched at the water's edge, washing his hands in the lake water.

"Messy business," he said when he'd felt her eyes on him and looked up.

She nodded.

July 26, 2000—4:15 P.M. _____

DOUG STOOD BEHIND ELIJAH AT his computer, reading over his shoulder. His stomach was clenched and his mouth felt cottony dry. The message was from a twelve-year-old American boy in Venezuela whose parents had been killed that morning when their truck, carrying emergency food supplies to a refugee camp, had struck a mine. The boy was alone at their headquarters with their computer, pleading for help.

"Enough," Doug said, touching Elijah's shoulder. He noticed a buzzing sensation in his ears. No, not a buzz, more like a low-pitched, almost-inaudible growl. "It's almost dinnertime. The boy's message is on the nets. The UN will be monitoring everything that comes out of the battle zone there—they'll have seen the message by now and sent help. He'll be okay." But even as he said it, swallowing to try to clear the sensation in his ears, Doug knew

133

what a stupid thing it was to say. *Okay*. He could almost taste the grief and fear behind the boy's words. "Just to be sure, I'll zap a copy of it to our consulate, or whatever we have there now."

"Doug!" Miranda called. "You've got to hear this."

"All right, we're just about done here." Doug swallowed again and rubbed at his ears. The growl faded and disappeared. "What's up?"

"Taryn was talking to that girl in Lithuania—Violeta—and when I put my hand on Taryn's shoulder, I got a mental picture of the room Violeta was in." Miranda rubbed her face with both hands and shook her head.

"It was the same picture I got," Taryn said. "Red rug with a flowered border, dark sofa, a table with carved legs—"

"And a samovar. From Lithuania! So far away, it's after midnight there."

Doug had pushed Elijah's chair, with him in it, to join the girls.

"Reaching," Taryn said.

"Through a computer," Miranda added.

"Violeta talks to trees," Taryn said. "I knew it even before she told me."

"And yesterday when Taryn was talking with Jacob in Jerusalem—"

"I got hot," Taryn said. "I thought our air conditioning was broken. But it wasn't ours; it was Jacob's."

"It's like thinking together. Too weird!"

Doug nodded, the message Elijah had found lying like a shadow across his mind. "Too weird."

Abby and Noah —
Watch your backs!
Harlan's out for blood.
No joke.
                    John

NOAH AND ABIGAIL STOOD ON the lawn, watching Harlan Turnbull, in camp shorts, safari shirt, and a straw hat, working the Visitors' Day crowd. He moved among the families scattered on towels, blankets, and lawn chairs along the strip of beach and up the lawn beneath the trees, shaking hands with parents, patting siblings on the head, applauding the efforts of young swimmers who splashed in the shallow water. Occasionally, he pulled an adult aside for a whispered conversation.

"You'd think he'd get tired of smiling," Abigail said.

"And you'd think they'd get tired of hearing the same old speech, especially since the ones he uses it on never see any change in their children from month to month." Noah shook his head. "Three parts justification for the lack of progress, one part vague hope."

"It's that last that makes it work," Abigail said.

Now Turnbull hurried to a man who had just arrived, trailing an entourage that included a uniformed chauffeur carrying folding chairs, along with a nanny shepherding Todd and a pair of twin girls. Todd, shaking his fingers in front of his eyes, stopped every few steps and had to be prodded to keep moving. Turnbull's smile had expanded, and he grasped the father's hand in both of his. "Like a dachshund greeting its owner," Abigail observed. "You can practically see his tail wagging!"

"Thomas Randolph," Noah said. "More money than Midas. And a son nobody can reach. Harlan told me yesterday that Randolph has agreed to fund his drug protocol—the one the

136

foundation turned down last spring as too speculative."

"Only one thing Harlan likes better than parents with money—*desperate* parents with money." Abigail smiled and waved at Mrs. Lasko, who was trying to keep Timmy from tearing out the grass along the edge of their blanket. "Has he mentioned Miranda to you lately?"

Noah shook his head. "No news is good news. We'd have heard by now if Deitz had given him any hope of getting her back. The only way he can save face is by avoiding the subject altogether—as if he's changed his mind. Or maybe by now he's convinced himself it was all his own idea."

"John's note makes me nervous. How do we watch our backs?"

"You know John's an alarmist," Noah said, "one step this side of paranoid. Harlan can be as angry as he wants. There's nothing he can do about it. Trust me. Our little family has nothing to fear from Harlan."

"I suppose you're right." Abigail looked to where Taryn and Elijah were sitting on the Ark family's quilt, spread out under an enormous white pine near the path to the house. They were side by side, Elijah turning his marble, Taryn looking out at the lake. "Our little family. I wish I understood what we've stumbled onto here."

Noah scratched his beard. "Whatever it is, if we could bottle it, we'd make a fortune. As it is, if we report it carefully, the GFGHP has to look like the idea of the century. The change in Elijah alone makes us look like miracle workers. John's boggled. At first he didn't believe me, but I showed him a printout of one of Elijah's online conversations. From a diagnosis of autism to full participation on the global networks in a matter of weeks. He interacts with other people, on the screen at least, like a normal eight-year-old. I take that back. Like an extremely above-normal eight-year-old." Noah nodded and waved to a family coming up from the beach to a cluster of chairs nearby. "He's been sharing incredible stories—adventure tales—with the violin prodigy from Jerusalem. He's invented his own country."

"Tondishi."

"Right. And Doug says already there's hardly anything the kid can't do with a computer. Doug's had to make an effort to stay ahead of him."

"I don't like what he finds when he just browses the networks," Abigail said. "It's like he's a magnet for violence. It wasn't so bad at first, when he was just finding those stories on the news services. At least they were no worse than an average newspaper. But with trillions of network interactions in the world every day, how does he find the other things? Not even the tabloids would print those. Did you see the piece he found yesterday afternoon? It was an eyewitness account—incredibly graphic—of a massacre in a place I'd never heard of. Some splinter of an Eastern European country that shattered a decade ago. Rape, murder, torture, dismemberment."

"I know," Noah said.

"Shouldn't we cut back on his time in the lab?"

"I told him to skip it yesterday, but he went anyway. I don't know if it's the computers he likes so much or just being with Doug. No sense making an issue of the violence unless we actually see that it's causing him problems."

"I dreamt about that massacre last night!" Abigail shook her

138

head. "What can it be doing to him? He's only eight years old. And the others, for that matter. Taryn reacted to those horror novels—only novels, only fiction—without even reading them. And Doug—"

"They're all managing to cope with it somehow. Maybe because most of what they're doing on the networks is so good for them. And having each other. Face it, my love. There really is a kind of miracle going on here. You can *feel* it, whatever it is." Doug and Miranda appeared on the path from the house with a picnic basket and a jug of lemonade. "Here comes lunch." Noah took Abigail's arm. "Let's go be parents."

Abigail sighed. "The only ones they have. You'd think Doug's could have managed to drive forty-five miles on a summer Saturday to visit the son they nearly lost."

"At least Miranda's parents have distance as an excuse. Their current workshop's in Seattle."

Abigail nodded to where Turnbull had taken Mr. Randolph down to the boathouse and was carrying on an enthusiastic conversation, gesturing toward the lake. "What do you bet he's offering to take the man fishing. Just what Visitors' Day is for—Daddy goes fishing while the servants watch the children."

"At least Daddy comes."

July 29, 2000 _____

MIRANDA AND DOUG HAD THE deep water to themselves after lunch. The few children who had gone back to the water splashed in the shallows. Miranda was stretched on her stomach on the raft, her chin resting on her doubled fists, watching Doug swim to the rope that marked the beginning of the deep water and back, over and over. His strokes were strong and steady, and she had given up waiting for him to tire.

The sound of a boat motor roaring to life turned her attention to the dock, where Turnbull and another man were getting ready to cast off. Miranda watched as the boat moved slowly away from the dock and then, well beyond the swimming area, picked up speed. Turnbull hadn't talked to Noah and Abigail before he went out in the boat, she thought. Odd.

She'd gone to the Ark after lunch to change into her bathing suit, and when she came out, Turnbull had been hurrying up the path. He'd jumped when he saw her, as if he hadn't been expecting anyone. His face had gone even pinker than usual and he spluttered a moment before explaining that he was looking for Noah and Abigail—something urgent to tell them, he said. She told him where they were, wondering why he hadn't been able to find them himself. They'd been right out on the lawn when she came to change. If what he had to tell them was so urgent, she thought now, why had he gone boating first?

The raft dipped suddenly as Doug, breathing hard, pulled himself out of the water. With a smooth, fluid movement he was standing by her shoulder, a pool of water steaming in the sun at his feet. Miranda shaded her eyes and looked up into the dark silhouette of his face. "You're good," she said. "I thought you were never going to stop."

He shook his head to drain the water from his ears. "Slow and steady. I could swim the lake and back if they'd let us. I don't get enough exercise here." He reached down and took hold of her upper arm, squeezing it playfully. "You either. Look at these flabby biceps!"

Miranda, feeling the warmth of his touch down her arm and into her chest, pulled free and sat up. "Beauty like mine doesn't need biceps."

"Are you speaking of intellectual beauty, Baby Genius?" Doug sat down next to her. She was aware of his presence, his closeness, as thoroughly as if their bodies were touching. "Because..." He tilted his head away from her and picked at the peeling paint of the raft. "Because...some people might say you have the other kind, too."

Before she could respond, he stretched out on his back and closed his eyes. Water droplets glistened in the dark curly hair on his legs and she watched his calf muscles move as he flexed his toes. "Aaah," he said, stretching. "At this moment, here on this raft, you could almost believe we were regular, ordinary people out in the regular, ordinary world."

Miranda reached to touch his ankle bracelet. "Except for this."

"Yeah." He turned his head to her and opened his eyes. "Do you realize this is the first time we have ever actually been alone together? In person instead of on computer screens? You and me and nobody else."

Her heartbeat was suddenly loud in her ears and she wondered if it could be heard over the water lapping at the raft. "Yes," she said. *Coup de foudre*—the French phrase came into her mind. She had read it in a novel somewhere. A thunderbolt, it meant. A visitation of sudden, overwhelming passion. She saw now that she had not truly understood the phrase.

"Of course, the lifeguards are watching our every move."

Miranda, still thinking of thunderbolts, blinked. "So," she said, "let's not move."

"Okay." He patted the raft next to him. "We'll just be two ordinary people sunbathing."

Miranda grinned. She stretched out next to him and closed her eyes. He shifted slightly and their arms were touching from elbow to shoulder. The heat of his skin against hers seemed suddenly more intense than the heat of the raft against her back. She had never felt this way before, as if her whole body were vibrating. Not vibrating—thrumming. She took a long, slow breath.

"We could try reaching," Doug said. "See if we can connect with the lake."

Miranda swallowed, aware that her heart had not slowed or quieted. "You mean like a competition? See who can do it first? Or best?"

"No. We do it together, and then compare notes to see if we got the same images."

"Okay. The lake." She forced her mind away from the heat where their arms touched, and tried to relax.

At first there was nothing except the dark orange of the sun through her eyelids. She took a breath and formed an image of the lake. Gradually it came, the lake as it looked from the lodge— smooth, calm water reflecting the sky, the mountain, the trees. She saw the beach, the line of buoys marking the deep water, the raft. On the raft the two of them. Suddenly Doug's lean, muscled body filled her mind, glistening in the sun, just as he had looked a moment before, flexing his toes. Her heart hammered even more insistently in her chest and she felt filled with light.

The image began to change, like a computer image morphing.

142

It was not Doug she was seeing now. It was herself. She saw her own closed eyes, the lashes dark against her cheeks. Long legs, long arms, the slight bulge of her breasts against her suit. She felt a tug in the very center of her being, a warm, dark, urgent pressure. And knew it was Doug's feeling that filled her, so like her own but sharper, more insistent. This, too, a thunderbolt.

Miranda sat up, breathing hard. Doug was leaning on one elbow and their eyes caught. Linked. Miranda looked away, concentrating on the peeling paint of the raft. "Well?" she said, trying to keep her voice steady.

"Sorry," Doug said. "I lost my concentration."

"Me too," she said. Whatever had happened, it was not something she could talk about. She was not sure she even wanted to think about it. *Imagination,* she told herself firmly. People just could not do what she thought she'd just done. And a good thing. A very good thing. Had he invaded her the way she—? She could not finish the thought.

She wanted him to look away. To move. To say something that would take them away from what had just happened. He did not.

She could feel his eyes like hands on her bare skin. When the pressure in her chest seemed too much to stand, she cleared her throat and spoke. "I had the dream again last night."

He sat up then and wrapped his arms around his knees. "What was happening?"

Miranda felt the change between them, the lessening of tension. She took a breath, as if she'd been swimming underwater a long time, feeling both relieved and somehow forsaken. Alone again. *Coup de foudre.* She remembered a shade of meaning—once it happened, it was irrevocable. Yes.

She looked up at the mountain. "Nothing really new. We were heading for the mountains. Fast. It was cold. For the first time the sweater the old woman gave me wasn't enough. I kept trying to wrap it tighter, but it wasn't enough. The sounds were getting closer behind us, and I knew we were running away from something. But I had a feeling we were running toward something, too."

Doug sat for a long time, his chin on his knees, before he spoke. "The quest."

Miranda nodded. "Whatever it is."

They watched a cloud shadow drift across Laurel Mountain's peak. "Mountains are just there," Doug said, "no matter what human beings do. Laurel Mountain must have looked exactly like that the first time the Europeans laid eyes on it."

"Maybe the first time humans laid eyes on it," Miranda said.

"Taryn's right and she's wrong."

"What do you mean?"

"About connecting." Doug ran his hand through his hair. "It helps to get a different sense of things, a mountain's long view, or a tree's. But it can't change what's happening. What humans are doing—Taryn's war at the end of the world."

Miranda didn't answer.

"Elijah pulls in violence. But it's never nature's violence—there was an earthquake in Mexico two days ago, and he didn't pull that off the news services. There were a gazillion messages on the nets afterward asking for help, offering it. You must have seen them. He didn't pull in a single one of those. Every terrible story he brings in is humans against humans. Some piece of Taryn's war."

144

"Like the bombing of the soccer stadium."

Doug nodded. "Terrorists. They want people scared so they'll give in to whatever the terrorists want. But the more fear there is, the more violence there is. What do people do when they're scared? They buy a gun. They're afraid of violence, so they buy a gun! I told you. It's bred in the bone."

Miranda squeezed her eyes shut. She felt the raft rocking gently beneath them, the sun on her head, on her back. And remembered. "The purple lion."

"What?"

She told him about her nightmare. "Freud said every character in your dreams is you. Do you think that's true? That lion was all claws and teeth and muscle. Was it the violence in me I was afraid of?"

Doug rubbed with his thumb at the scar on his left wrist. "Could be."

"But Doug, the lion didn't win. He came back and back and back, and then he was gone." Miranda tried to remember what had happened to that nightmare, what had finally made it stop. She couldn't. It had been there and then it had been gone. "Somehow, somewhere along the line, the lion must have lost! Somehow I drove him out."

Doug shook his head. "You didn't drive him out. You just got him chained down. Freud would tell you that. You got old enough to learn the rules. And the rules chained him down. But for humans rules are recent history. And they break. So do chains." Doug pushed himself to his feet and stood for a moment, staring at the mountain. "*Homo horribilis*. That lion's still there. At the center of everything." Doug dove into the water and began stroking toward the beach, leaving Miranda rocking alone on the raft.

TARYN, SITTING AT THE WATER'S EDGE, shivered and drew her towel closer around her. The sun was slipping toward the mountains and the air had cooled. Noah and Abigail, Miranda and Doug were playing a game of Trivial Pursuit up on the quilt, and Elijah was sitting near them, watching. Listening.

No one was in the water now. Some families had already gone home, and the noise and confusion of the others had moved back and away from the water's edge. The swallows that nested in the eaves of the lodge had stayed far from the beach all day. But now they were back, swooping and gliding over the surface of the lake, their wings occasionally making ripples where they touched. Taryn watched them, reveling in their sudden turns, their dives and climbs.

The hum of a boat engine slipped into her awareness and grew louder. After a moment, she watched the swallows wheel and soar away as Harlan Turnbull's boat came knifing through the water, kicking up waves and leaving a trail of turbulence behind. The boat roared closer, the engine slowing as it drew near. It rode a swell from behind as Turnbull cut the engine and guided the boat's long glide to the wooden dock that stretched into the water between the boathouse and the swimming area. When it bumped the dock, Turnbull and the man who was with him looped lines around cleats on the dock's edge. Both were

146

smiling broadly as they clambered out, balancing fishing poles.

Turnbull squatted and unhooked a thin braided yellow line that stretched from a cleat on the side of the boat down into the water, and Taryn saw the reason for their smiles. He pulled the stringer free of the water; three large golden-bellied fish struggled at the end, the line looped through their mouths and flaring gills. As they rose into the sunlight, the fish flapped powerful tails, trying vainly to push against the air, to loose themselves and swim away. They opened mouths and gills, gasping for breath.

Taryn's chest hurt with the effort of the fishes' silent flailing. Without thinking, she leapt to her feet, her towel falling to the wet sand, and ran through the shallow water toward the dock. Turnbull handed the stringer to the other man, then reached into the boat and pulled out a Styrofoam cooler, which he set on the dock.

"No," Taryn yelled as she scrambled onto the end of the dock. "No!" She hurled herself toward the men. Turnbull caught her arm as she tried to get past him, tried to grab the stringer that the man, surprised by her attack, was holding aloft now. "Let them go," she yelled, fighting to break free.

Turnbull held fast, grabbing for her other arm as she struggled to reach the fish, struggled to breathe around the agony that was searing her own lungs.

"You don't need them," she shouted at the man, who had backed out of range now. "Let them go!"

Turnbull had caught her fully now, was holding her by both arms, his fingers digging into her skin. "Control yourself," he said between clenched teeth, his voice low and intense as she tried to break away. He looked over her head, and his voice

147

changed completely as he spoke. "It's all right. I have her."

Taryn continued to fight the grip of Turnbull's hands as the man took the lid from the cooler and began to loosen the stringer's loop. The fish went on flapping their tails, more slowly now, their mouths working. Taryn could feel darkness rising. "Let them go!" she said again.

The man stopped what he was doing and looked at her. "They're only fish," he said, showing them to her as if she didn't know, as if these lives couldn't possibly matter. "Only fish."

Taryn went still in Turnbull's hands. "If you don't let them go by yourself, I'll make you do it."

The man laughed.

"You'll what?" Turnbull's grip tightened. "You'll *make* him? We'll see about that." He dragged her away and marched her ahead of him down the dock.

She twisted so that she could keep the man in sight. "I mean it," she yelled back. "I can do it. I can do it!"

When they reached the grass at the end of the dock, Turnbull stopped. His pink face smiled down at her, his eyes mocking as he called to the man, "I think you're safe enough now."

The man bent over the cooler, removed the stringer, and dropped the fish inside.

Taryn closed her eyes and let her mind go quiet. She could no longer feel the pressure on her arms, the grass beneath her bare feet. She built a picture in her mind and focused on it. Focused.

"Hey!" The man's voice broke her concentration. "Hey, hey, hey! Ow!"

She opened her eyes, to see swallows swooping and diving at

the man, their wings brushing his head as they passed. He dropped the empty stringer, and it slid off the dock and into the water. The swallows dove, coming in from left and right, in front and behind, striking at his head now with their beaks. He ducked and dodged, shielding his head with his hands, and still the birds swooped. Bright spots of red appeared on his hands, on his forehead where a bird hit him while he flailed at the others. He snatched the cooler and upended it. The fish slapped back into the water with a splash, and he held the empty cooler like a helmet over his head as he hurried off the dock. The swallows kept swooping as he moved, jolting the cooler in his hands, until he had reached the grass. Then, circling once, so that Turnbull, still holding Taryn, ducked as well, the birds flew off across the water and disappeared.

Taryn felt her lungs expand as the fish paused in the dark water beneath the dock, sucking water over and through their gills. After a moment they moved; with a stroke of their tails, they were gone. She took a long breath, looked up at the man, and smiled.

"Good Lord!" he said to Turnbull as he set down the cooler. "Have you ever seen anything like that?" He dug a handkerchief out of his pocket and wiped blood from his forehead and the backs of his hands. "Like something out of Hitchcock!" He laughed a short, dry laugh. "I...ah...if I didn't know better, I'd think this kid had made good on her threat."

Turnbull's fingers closed more tightly on Taryn's arms, and she gasped in pain. "Those birds'll do that," he said. "There must have been a swarm of gnats above you out there, or mosquitoes. It's about that time of day."

The man turned and looked back along the dock. "I suppose. Still…"

Abigail was there then. "It's all right, Harlan," she was saying, "I'll take Taryn. You go in with Mr. Randolph and check out those wounds…get some antiseptic on them." She turned to Randolph. "No sense taking a chance with some kind of infection. Wild birds, you know. You must have been standing in a swarm of bugs out there."

Turnbull, still gripping Taryn's arms, looked from Randolph to Abigail. "Just what I said."

"I'm sorry about Taryn's behavior," Abigail said to Randolph. "She cares terrifically about animals. All animals, even fish. And it's been a long day. She's tired."

Taryn smiled into Abigail's eyes as Turnbull loosened his grip. She *was* tired, she realized. Very, very tired. Abigail took her hand, and she felt Turnbull let go, the blood moving again through her arms, where his fingers had left marks.

As she and Abigail walked away, Taryn could feel Turnbull's gaze burning like a flame against her back.

From the Desk of
HARLAN TURNBULL, M.D., Ph.D.

MEMO: To Noah and Abigail Periodes
COPY: Harold Deitz, President of the Board
FROM: HT
RE: Taryn Forrester
DATE: July 29, 2000

Taryn Forrester's physical attack today on the parent of another
patient is a disturbing behavioral change in a patient who has
previously been docile and somewhat withdrawn.

Even more disturbing is her obvious belief that she caused the sudden
appearance of the birds, whose normal feeding behavior coincidentally
resulted in Mr. Randolph's losing the fish she had threatened to
release. This suggests a recurrence (and possible deepening) of the
delusional pattern noted by the aunt who brought her to us more than a
year ago. Her file indicates that today's incident is the first
evidence of delusion since she began treatment at Laurel Mountain. The
move to the GFGHP, far from creating an improvement in this patient,
appears to be causing a quite serious regression.

As medical director, I must express deep concern; continuing the
current treatment (or lack thereof—I note that she has been taken off
her medication) could result in irreparable harm to this patient.

From the Desk of
ABIGAIL PERIODES, Ph.D.

To: Harlan Turnbull, M.D. Ph.D.
FROM: Abigail Periodes
COPY: Harold Deitz, President of the Board
RE: Taryn Forrester
DATE: July 29, 2000

Noah and I share your concern, Harlan, with Taryn's response to seeing you and Mr. Randolph with the catch from your Visitors' Day fishing trip. As you may not know, Taryn is a passionate defender of animal life. Her behavior, though inappropriate to the occasion, can certainly be considered no worse than the behavior of apparently "sane" adults who throw red paint on the fur coats of pedestrians on New York City sidewalks. We have spoken with her about the best way to handle her feelings in the future.

As for a delusion about causing the appearance of the swallows (or their behavior), we don't quite understand where this idea came from. I heard Mr. Randolph joke that if he didn't know better, he'd have believed Taryn had made good on her threat to force him to put the fish back. But, of course, he did know better. As far as we can determine, the only one who has suggested a connection between Taryn's wish to save the lives of three fish and the swallows' feeding pattern is you yourself.

Taryn is an extremely precocious and sensitive child. I don't know what her psychological condition may have been when she was being required to participate in her mother's unusual "church." However, I can assure you that there is absolutely no evidence that Taryn Forrester has any delusions about her capabilities at this time.

OVER HER SHOULDER, NOAH READ the memo Abigail was printing out, and laughed. "We could take a lie-detector test on that last statement."

Abigail nodded. "But is it going to satisfy Harlan? Is his copying Deitz with this attack just revenge for taking Miranda away from him, or is it the first volley in a new assault?"

Noah shrugged. "Same objective, different tactic. He wants to shake Deitz's faith in the project. He didn't succeed focusing on Miranda, so he's trying a new way."

"But can he?"

"You know Harold as well as I do. What do you think?"

"I was hoping for some reassurance. If he goes after us on medical grounds—"

"We're unassailable on medical grounds," Noah said. "We have an essentially cured autistic child, a vandal become global citizen, and four 'sick' kids interacting successfully with each other and daily on the nets. He doesn't have a leg to stand on!"

ELIJAH, HOT AND SWEATY FROM their after-chapel walk, held his marble in a bit of sun that filtered through the branches overhead. He turned it, watching the blue-and-white interior change, aware of Doug, next to him, picking a fresh blade of grass to stretch between his thumbs for a whistle. Elijah was aware, too, of Taryn leaning against the tree, Miranda watching the game two weekend aides had organized for the patients from the lodge. As he turned the marble, feeling the familiar surface between his fingers, Elijah realized that something inside himself had changed. He couldn't get inside the marble anymore, couldn't shut off all sensation, protecting himself with the thick layer of clear glass that protected the blue-and-white swirl. Even sounds from the game on the lawn intruded. He looked up now, his attention caught.

Two teams of children faced each other across a net, the smaller ones in front, the larger ones in rows behind. Elijah could see the point of the game—one team would hit a bright beach ball over the net and the other team was supposed to hit it back. But it wasn't going well. Almost every time the ball was hit there would be an argument of some kind. The low growl that was always in Elijah's head when lodge children were nearby had grown louder, more intrusive.

A tall boy with a shadow of mustache hit the ball. It went into the net instead of over it, and the boy began swearing, protesting that the ball was too light. At the same time Timmy, the boy who had smashed the computer, yelled that nobody ever hit it to him. A dark-haired girl picked up the ball, and Timmy tried to take it away from her. When she held on, he kicked her again and again until she let go, screaming at the top of her lungs. The growl had grown nearly as loud now as the girl's screams.

Timmy tried to hit the ball over the net, but one of the aides grabbed him by one arm and dragged him away. He sat Timmy down on the grass away from the game and went off to get the ball, which two others now were fighting over.

The game, Elijah thought, had gone completely *pturflukt,* as Miranda would say. Four children were leaping for the ball the

154

aide was holding above his head, and the other aide, her face red, was leaning over the girl Timmy had kicked, trying to get her to stop crying. A couple of the older patients wandered away.

The growl grew steadily louder in Elijah's head, and a shrill whistle pierced the air. "Everybody sit!" the aide who had blown the whistle yelled. "Whoever can sit still for five minutes gets a treat!" One by one the children on both sides of the net sat down.

Suddenly, Elijah felt a deep vibration that moved through his body as if it were coming from the ground beneath him. It reminded him of how it felt to sit on the dryer at the Laundromat, waiting for the clothes to be done. Steady. Insistent. He put a hand down on the grass. The vibration was not in the ground. Like the growl, it was coming from inside himself. Like the growl, he understood, it was a warning. Not of what was already happening, but of something considered. Intended.

Willing the vibration to stop, Elijah closed his eyes. An image of Timmy Lasko filled his mind, and Elijah understood him the way he understood the characters he made up for his Tondishi stories. He knew what Timmy wanted. Elijah began to moan.

Doug, sitting next to Elijah, felt a chill up his spine as the sound began. He dropped the grass blade he had been using for a whistle and looked up. The aides, their heads together, their backs to the children, were conferring. As Elijah's voice grew louder, Doug saw Timmy Lasko creeping up from behind a patch of tall grass near the beach, bent over with the weight of a fat white rock he had taken from the line of boundary stones. The boy was moving stealthily but fast, his eyes focused on the little girl he had

155

fought with, who sat facing the other way, a few feet in front of him.

Doug saw what Timmy intended to do. Already, the boy was struggling to lift the rock higher. Elijah's moan became a wail. Doug put a hand on Elijah's shoulder. At the same moment he felt Taryn take his other hand as she reached to touch Miranda's arm.

As the contact was made between the four of them, Doug had a sensation unlike anything he had ever felt before. It was as if he could feel every organ and bone, every cell in his body—as if each had its own consciousness. Through Elijah's shoulder he seemed to feel his, too, then Taryn's, and finally Miranda's. The whole awareness tingled, as if a surge of electricity had begun flowing between them.

Timmy, directly behind the girl now, lifted the rock as high as he could above the girl's head.

No! Doug didn't know whether he had shouted the word or only thought it, but the sound seemed to reverberate in his head as he felt energy pulse through him. The scene in front of him stopped, like a broken piece of film, the edges blurring. Timmy, in slow motion, staggered. With a bewildered frown, he looked up at the rock in his hands, then began to bring it down, slowly, deliberately, with fierce intensity. At last he opened his hands and let it go. The rock seemed to hover in the air a moment before it began its slow fall toward Timmy's sandaled foot. Doug heard the crunch of breaking bones, saw the bright spray of blood.

As if the film had slipped back to normal speed, everything began to move. Timmy screamed, the aides ran toward him, other children leapt up, joining Timmy's screams.

WHEN TARYN KNOCKED ON THE others' doors to wake them at the hour they had agreed to meet, they had been ready, as if an internal alarm had coordinated their waking. Now they sat in a tight circle, their chairs rolled as close together as they could get. Taryn looked from one to another, their faces still clouded with sleep.

"We did that to Timmy," she said. "We smashed his foot."

"We didn't!" Miranda protested. "The rock was too heavy for him, and he dropped it, that's all."

"He didn't just drop it. *He did to himself what he meant to do to Jemma.*"

Doug rubbed his face with both hands, as if pushing away the last muzziness of sleep. His eyes had come thoroughly awake. "Do you mean that...energy surge, or whatever it was, 'reflected' what he meant to do? Bounced his intention back at him?"

Taryn nodded.

Elijah looked up from his marble, and his eyes caught Taryn's. *Yes,* they said.

Doug frowned. Taryn watched a muscle in his jaw move as he relived the morning's event in his mind, instant by instant. She relived it with him. At last he nodded and turned to Miranda. "She's right. Think about it. Like putting a mirror in front of a laser beam. She's right."

"That's impossible."

Taryn was certain that Miranda understood. Understood but didn't want to. "It happened," she said quietly. "You felt it."

"But—"

"It's no worse than the Heisenberg uncertainty in physics. Or the Banach-Tarski paradox in math," Doug said. "We don't know enough to say what's impossible."

"The what paradox?"

"Banach-Tarski. If set theory works the way mathematicians would like it to, you could cut a sphere into pieces and then reassemble the pieces—*the same pieces*—into a sphere twice as big."

Miranda shook her head. "That's math? The subject you said was so clean and pretty? So predictable?"

Doug nodded, grinning. "It's the kind of math most mathematicians wish would go away." His face grew serious. "Look. What happened this morning isn't any stranger than that. It isn't any stranger than gravity, if you think about it. We don't really understand what gravity is, but we know it's real."

Taryn could read the excitement in Doug's eyes as his mind worked. "We must never do what we did this morning again!"

"But we didn't *do* anything," Miranda said. "It just happened."

"Then we have to make sure it never happens again."

"Why?" Doug asked.

"Because we hurt Timmy terribly."

Doug smacked the arms of his chair. "No we didn't. *Timmy* hurt Timmy. All we did was turn his violent intentions back on him." Doug pushed back his chair and stood up. His face seemed lit from within as he paced behind them, tracing in words the path his thoughts had taken. "*This* is the quest! What we're here to do. It's why we have no weapons in the dream. We don't need them." He waved toward a metal basket next to the printers, where the stories Elijah had pulled from the networks were stacked. "Look what those stories are telling us about the world. Armageddon. If we're mutations, the important difference isn't super-intelligent brains—some of the best brains humanity ever produced created the most terrible weapons. What's important is this thing we did today, reflecting violence back on the person who would use it against someone else. It just happened today, but what if we learned to use it, control it? Think what that would mean!"

"Timmy had a rock," Taryn said. "What if it had been a gun?"

Doug waved the question away. "What if? Whatever level of violence a person is willing to use, that level of violence would come back to him. In the Bible it says, 'As ye sow, so shall ye reap.' That's exactly what it would be. No more, no less. Violent intentions would only hurt the person who had them in the first place. It's so elegant. If enough people could do what we did today, then anyone who tried to kill someone else would be killed. Violence would destroy itself, eat itself up and be gone from the world!"

"No!" Taryn said. This was the problem she had found. The impossible problem. "Don't you see? We've done it now. We know what happens. It could never 'just happen' again, never be an accident. We couldn't reflect violence without intending it ourselves! Reflecting it *is* an act of violence. Violence wouldn't be gone from the world. It would be *in us!*"

For a long moment, the only sounds were the faint humming of the computers and the movement of Doug's bare feet on the tile floor as he paced.

"We've found something important," Doug said, his voice tight. He stood still for a moment. "This has to be why we're dreaming together. Why we're here, our connection. *This* is the

159

new thing that's in us. We can't ignore it. We can't just throw it away!"

"We can't do violence, either," Taryn said.

Doug turned on her. "You want us connecting with mountains, trees, your precious nature. Well, just think about nature for a minute. Animals killing and eating each other, tornadoes, hurricanes, earthquakes. What if that mountain out there was a volcano? If it erupted—just doing what its own internal reality dictated—it would kill all life as close to it as we are now. That's violence. *Natural* violence. What's the difference?"

Taryn sat very still, searching for the answer she knew had to be there. She found it. "The difference is that we would know. For us, it would be a choice."

July 31, 2000—5:15 P.M. _____

WHILE THEIR DINNER BAKED, SENDING the aroma of onion and garlic through the house, the family had gathered in the living room for the meeting Doug had requested. The four of them had spent the afternoon planning it, discovering connections they hadn't known about before. Now, with the tape recorder running, Doug, Miranda, and Taryn were doing their best to describe to Noah and Abigail everything that had led up to what had happened yesterday on the lawn.

Miranda told of the dream she had had, the man with the pummeling fists, the woman cowering behind, and another dream, of being pushed by older brothers from a tree house, breaking an arm. Doug told of a dream in Paris, looking out a window over the roofs of Montmartre, of another where he had stood in candlelight, surrounded by a group of people, his hands on a child's burning forehead, as the fever drained into his fingers and the skin cooled. Elijah had printed out a dream that afternoon, and Doug read it aloud—Elijah standing in a gloomy office with a heavy book clutched in both arms. He had been a girl in the dream, wearing a red dress, nose pressed against the window, watching children play on a jungle gym. The little girl would not go outside. She knew the children would only drive her away, calling her names, as they had done before. And Taryn described what only she had experienced awake, the memory of a cold, lonely night with a dead deer. "We're dreaming each other's memories," Miranda said when Taryn had finished.

Noah shook his head and rubbed at his beard. "I've been digging through all the psychic research I can get my hands on, looking for an explanation of just the little bit Abigail and I have seen happening here. Hermit thrushes appearing on windowsills, swallows diving at a person's head, simultaneous mental imagery. I didn't find any explanations. I did find a lot about dreams in the literature. Precognitive dreams, clairvoyant dreams, astral projections." He ticked them off on his fingers. "Apparently, these are considered pretty ordinary. But dreaming someone else's memories?"

"It isn't just memories," Miranda said. "We're dreaming a dream together, too. Recurring and progressive." She and Taryn and Doug took turns telling the dream.

Abigail put down her needlepoint. "I've heard of identical twins sharing a single dream, but the four of you—"

"It isn't just us," Taryn said. This was something they had

learned for certain that very day. "Last week Jacob, the violin prodigy from Jerusalem, told me about a dream that was so like ours I asked him if anyone else he knew was dreaming it with him. Two students from his music academy are in it. One's a six-year-old piano prodigy and the other's a teenager who wants to be a composer. He was afraid they'd think he was crazy if he asked them about it. They didn't. He told me today—they're dreaming it, too."

"And Violeta," Miranda said, "in Lithuania. The chess champion from her school is in a dream she's been having, so she asked him, and he's not only dreaming it, he knows one of the characters in the dream that Violeta doesn't know—his cousin. He's going to ask her, but we don't have the answer yet."

"And Akeylah—," Taryn began.

Abigail broke in. "Are you saying what these other children are dreaming is the same dream you four are having?"

"Close enough," Miranda said. "They're like fairy tales from different cultures—you know, the same basic story line with a few differences. We're headed for mountains; the Lithuanian kids are in a forest."

"Jacob's group is in the desert."

"And in all of them there are guns in the background," Doug said. "Or bombs. Or fire. Getting closer."

"Armageddon," Taryn said.

"Armageddon?" Abigail asked.

Taryn explained her mother's theory.

Noah drummed his fingers on the arm of the couch as she spoke. Then, very slowly, he nodded. "I think I can almost believe that."

162

"Everybody who's dreaming the dream has the same feeling—that we're on some kind of quest," Miranda said. "There's something we're supposed to be doing, and we need to find out what that is."

"Incredible." Noah looked at Abigail and she nodded. "What do you suppose we could call this? A nonlocal—asynchronous—shared mythological quest dream!"

"It's one for the books," Abigail said, "except for the small detail that no one would believe it."

A breeze blew through the living room from the porch, and rain spattered on the windows. For a long time they sat in silence as the rain began to fall harder.

"That isn't all," Taryn said at last. They hadn't been sure whether they dared to tell it all at once. But they needed to get to the rest of it.

Now they explained the events of the previous day that had sent Timmy Lasko to the hospital. Noah and Abigail sat unmoving, except for Abigail's left foot, which had begun tapping as if to music only she could hear. When they had finished, the rain had stopped, but the wind had picked up and was moving through the woods with the muted roar of a distant waterfall.

"So," Doug said, "we have two questions. First—do you believe it? That whatever happened between us out there, it turned Timmy's intention back on him?"

Abigail turned to Noah. "It was a big rock. Surely, it was just too heavy for him—"

"That's what everybody thought," Noah said. "But I went with him to the hospital. His foot was so badly injured, the doctor said it looked like someone had smashed it down on his foot deliberately. When I assured him that no one had touched the rock but Timmy, he did a bone-density test to see if Timmy's bones could be unusually brittle. They aren't."

Abigail sighed. She picked at the yarn at the back of her needlepoint. Then she turned to Doug. "When you played that piece for us—'Northern Lights'—were you thinking of them again while you played?"

"Not thinking, exactly. But seeing them in my mind."

She turned to the others. "Were you all seeing them?" Miranda and Taryn nodded. After a moment Elijah did, too. "I got them, too. So did Noah. Whatever the connections are between you, they were already strong enough to give us—to send us—the northern lights."

"We saw and heard the hermit thrush," Noah said.

Abigail looked at Taryn. "You *called* it, didn't you? And the swallows?"

Taryn shook her head. "I didn't call them, exactly. It was more like...an invitation. They didn't have to come."

"But they did. And the swallows did what you wanted done." She closed her eyes for a moment, her frown intensifying, and then opened them again. "We couldn't prove any of these things. But I've seen them. Felt them. And we've both felt something happening between you. I don't have explanations, can't even imagine what they could be. But...yes, I believe you."

Noah sighed and rubbed at his beard, this time with both hands. "Back to the psychic research. I'd like to have at least a glimmer of science behind some of this. Still, just now, and just between us family members, I believe you, too."

Abigail smiled grimly. "The stuffy psychological journals will

164

be falling over each other trying to be the first to print *this* study!"

"Sure," Noah said. "Just after they drum us out of the American Psychological Association."

Elijah, leaning against Doug's legs, began to moan.

July 31, 2000—5:48 P.M. _____

As Doug reached to put a hand on Elijah's shoulder there was a knock at the door. Harlan Turnbull pulled open the screen and stuck his head in. "Why would they drum you out of the APA? Mind if we come in? It smells good in here."

Noah clicked off the tape recorder as he stood. "You know the project plan, Harlan. No visitors until—"

Turnbull opened the door the rest of the way and held it as a tall, distinguished-looking man with a thick shock of unruly white hair stepped inside, smoothing his hair into place. "Quite a wind kicking up out there," said Harold Deitz, president of the board. "Highly irregular to drop in without warning, I know—" Abigail had started to get up, but he waved her back to her seat. "I was meeting with Harlan about something else and just couldn't leave without taking a peek at the new project. I persuaded him, I'm afraid. I promise we won't stay long."

Noah, his face stony, took the man's proffered hand as briefly as possible.

Abigail gave Noah a warning look and smiled warmly. "It isn't that we aren't glad to see you, Harold; it's just that the point of the group home is to create a safe—"

"—a safe, secure, and intimate family atmosphere," Turnbull

165

finished for her. "We know. Just think of us as extended family members who dropped by for a quick visit."

Doug patted Elijah, who was rocking at his feet, still moaning, and stood up. "I'm Doug McAllister," he said to Deitz. He gestured at the others. "Miranda Ellenby, Taryn Forrester, and"—he touched Elijah's head and the boy stopped rocking—"Elijah Raymond. New people scare him," he explained.

"Especially new men," Miranda added.

"Pleased to meet you all." Deitz nodded to Doug. "I understand you're the computer expert. I dropped in mainly to see the lab in operation. Maybe if we weren't here in the same room with him—" He glanced at Elijah, whose moaning had grown louder.

"Sure," Doug said. He led the two men down the hall. Noah followed.

"There's not much to see," Noah said, as they filed into the lab after Doug. Screen savers moved on the monitors and a printer hummed in the corner as it spit pages of copy into its tray.

"That's a record of all the network interactions from this afternoon," Doug explained. "We print hard copy for an additional backup."

Deitz leaned to touch a keyboard and the screen saver blinked off. "Are all the connections working? We had the devil's own time getting the fiber-optic lines laid this far out."

Doug caught Noah's eye and answered with a straight face. "The connections are great. Unusually so."

"The only thing that stops us is the weather," Noah said. "This afternoon Taryn was talking to a girl in Detroit, daughter of a professor at Wayne State, when the connection went dead. Storms in the Midwest—"

"Lightning strike," Doug said. "The university's whole system went down. Taryn had just asked her a question that was really important. I tried the rest of the afternoon to connect again but never could. Frustrating."

"Modern technology," Deitz said. "No matter how much you spend on it, you still can't beat Mother Nature." He looked around the room and nodded. "Looks like everything's up and running otherwise. I'm not enough of a technophile to understand all that you have here. What do you think, Harlan?"

Turnbull shrugged. "I wouldn't mind having some of it at the lodge."

Deitz laughed. "Do what they did. Get yourself a research grant! So. What do you think, Doug McAllister? Is this global family project working?"

"If you mean are we making global connections, sure. Taryn's been talking to kids all over the world. I'm in a math and chaos-theory conference. And music. Miranda translates so we can interact with anybody who doesn't know English."

"And the other boy—Elijah? Does he make connections this way, too?"

Doug glanced at the basketful of Elijah's printouts and nodded, a frown creasing his forehead. "Probably more than the rest of us put together."

"It turns out Elijah's a born computer whiz," Noah said. "Something of a prodigy, in fact. Are we done in here?"

Deitz nodded and went out as Noah held the door. Turnbull took a long look around and followed.

When they returned to the living room, Taryn had taken Doug's place on the couch. Elijah was leaning against her legs. He rolled his marble in his hand, his moaning almost too soft to be heard.

"Sorry to hear about the lightning in Detroit," Deitz said to Taryn. "It must have been frustrating not to be able to get the answer to your question."

Taryn looked up at him, a puzzled expression on her face.

"The question you had just asked the girl in Detroit when the system went down," he reminded her.

"Oh, that. She answered it later."

Deitz turned to Doug. "Later? I thought you said—"

"Dinner's just about ready," Abigail called from the kitchen. "Doug, would you help Miranda set the table?" She came into the room, wiping her hands on a towel. "Sorry there isn't enough to offer you dinner," she said to Turnbull and Deitz, "but you might not appreciate it, anyway. It's a casserole Taryn and Noah invented, and I won't make any guarantees. We've gone vegetarian."

"Vegetarian?" Turnbull asked. "I don't remember that in the project plan."

"Not to worry, Harlan," Abigail said. "It's all nutritionally sound."

Noah's tight smile was barely visible beneath the bush of his mustache. "Menus weren't in the project plan, Harlan. We're a family. We make that kind of decision together."

"We take turns cooking," Taryn said, "and I got sick when I smelled raw meat. I could feel how the animal died. Fear and pain and blood—"

Miranda, who had come in from the kitchen, interrupted. "When she told us how she felt, the rest of us could almost imagine it, too. So we decided none of us would eat meat."

168

"And we've been vegetarian since," Abigail finished.

"Well, we don't want to delay your dinner." Deitz shook Abigail's hand. "Thanks for letting us barge in like this."

"You're welcome. Come again"—she paused—"when the adjustment period we asked for is up."

Deitz nodded. "I'm sure I will. Maybe you'll have me to dinner. My wife would owe you a debt of gratitude if you could win me away from steak and potatoes." He turned to Doug. "Thanks for showing us the lab. I hope you get in touch with the folks in Detroit soon." He turned toward the door.

"Their system's back up now," Taryn said. "We'll be able to connect after dinner."

Deitz turned back, his eyebrows raised in surprise.

"Taryn's an optimist," Doug said. "I hope she's right this time."

Turnbull pointed at the tape recorder on the coffee table. "How much of the 'family' interaction do you put on tape?"

"Just formal meetings," Abigail said. "The rest of our life here—"

Elijah's moan, which had been rising in volume, became a high, sharp wail.

Abigail hurried Turnbull to the door and held it open for the two men to leave. "This is why we wanted to discourage visitors," she said, following them onto the porch. "We want the children to have a sense of absolute security in this house. Now that Elijah's begun to reach out to the world he's particularly vulnerable. As Miranda said, he's terrified of unfamiliar men. Not surprising, given his history." She had to raise her voice to be heard over the wind and the sound of Elijah's keening.

When Turnbull and Deitz had disappeared in the direction of the lodge, she went back inside. Noah stood at the window, staring down the empty pathway, his face red against the white of his beard. "That was no spur-of-the-moment visit," he said.

Elijah's wailing softened, fading slowly until the room was quiet, only an echo seeming to catch in the corners. He raised his head, looking from one to another, making eye contact. An image of Harlan Turnbull formed in their heads.

"He wants to hurt us," Elijah said. Before anyone could react to the sound of his voice, he spoke again. "He wants to shut down the Ark."

Storm Rising

Journal—Miranda Ellenby
July 31, 2000—10:50 P.M.

Noah and Abigail say not to worry. Turnbull can't shut us down. It isn't that the threat Elijah senses from him isn't real, only that it's what Turnbull wants to do, not what he CAN do. They say the board spent so much of the foundation's money on this project they wouldn't shut it down so soon.

Besides, if Turnbull really challenges what's going on here, Elijah, now that he's talking—TALKING!—is our ace in the hole. With the changes that have happened for Elijah since he came here, how can anybody say the Ark isn't working? And you don't shut down what's working.

Still, Doug's planning to get into Turnbull's private computer files (some morning when he's helping out at the lodge lab) and see what he's planning. He got Turnbull's password back when he was hacking over there before he came to the Ark. It's NOBEL. It would be funny if it wasn't so pathetic.

July 31, 2000—11:20 P.M. _____

"I DON'T WANT TO TALK about it anymore," Abigail said, pulling the covers up to her chin. "If I go to sleep and dream about riding a horse toward a mountain…"

Noah, who was sitting up against his pillows, writing notes in his notebook computer, shrugged. "It would seem that you and I don't have whatever it takes to participate in the dream. If it's a mutation, we don't have it. Anyway, except for the question of

173

age, I prefer to think we're the old man and the old woman, just here to give them what they need for their quest."

"Quest! I can't get out of my mind the damage that rock did to Timmy's foot. There's a touch of poetic justice about it, of course. But this is the first time they've done this—whatever it is. What else could they do?"

"And what about the others? You heard what Taryn told them about getting the answer to the question she asked Akeylah—she had to have gotten the answer when the computers were still down. Taryn, at least, seems to be able to make the global connections without the services of the electronic highway."

"Taryn. The child who can *invite* swallows to attack a fisherman. We can't publish this, Noah."

"No. I don't see how we can. We'll record it. We'll write it up. But the field of psychology isn't ready for these kids."

"A physicist once said, 'If you understand quantum physics and aren't boggled by it, you don't understand quantum physics.'"

Noah closed his laptop. "Physics has the cloak of hard science to give it credibility. We don't. Unless we can figure out a way to reproduce what they're doing in a laboratory setting, so others can replicate it, all we have is what the kids tell us and our own subjective experience. Convincing enough to us, worthless as far as science is concerned."

August 1, 2000—11:00 A.M. _____

ELIJAH AND TARYN WERE WORKING at their terminals and Miranda was sitting at the printer table, reading a long message in German

174

she was preparing to translate, when Doug arrived in the lab after his session with Noah. Taryn looked up when he came in. "Have you made any contacts in Northern Ireland?" she asked. "You or Noah or Abigail?"

Doug shook his head. "Why?"

"Because we got a message this morning from a brother and sister in Belfast. Their names are Liam and Siobhan. He's eleven and she's eight. Their father designs computer software and their house is probably equipped as well as this lab. They're both pretty famous there because she's played violin with the symphony and he's had a showing of his paintings in a gallery. The message was kind of an introduction, and they asked us to write back and tell them who we are."

"How did they find us?"

Taryn shrugged. "They didn't say. I thought maybe you'd made a contact that would explain it."

"The only contacts we have so far in the British Isles are in London and Edinburgh, and the Edinburgh one's a psychologist Abigail knows."

"Maybe they found us the way Elijah finds what he finds every time he goes out on the nets. He gets drawn to violence, and they got drawn to us."

Miranda put down the pages she'd been reading. "Drawn to us?"

Taryn, frowning, nodded. "I've been thinking that whatever brought us together here, whatever's giving us our dream and the others theirs, must be working out beyond what we're aware of. There have to be kids like us that we don't know about. Maybe kids that nobody knows about. What if the more of us we find and connect with, the stronger the connections get, until they begin to work like a magnet, sort of, pulling others in?"

"Something like critical mass," Doug said.

"Look at this." Taryn touched a few keys. "Liam sent a photo of one of his paintings."

Doug and Miranda came to stand over her shoulder. A picture came up on her screen and they gasped. It was a landscape, painted in bold colors. Though there was something abstract about it, there was no mistaking the subject. It was their own lake, as it appeared from the porch of the lodge. There were the two ridges of mountains meeting at the end and, rising behind, Laurel Mountain, complete with the cap of clouds it so often wore.

"I don't suppose there could be a place that looks exactly like Laurel Mountain in Northern Ireland," Doug said. "What did he say about it?"

"That it was an image that came into his mind—so strongly he had to paint it. He thought we might be interested in seeing it."

"When did he do it?" Miranda asked.

"He only said it was his newest piece."

Doug squinted at the image on Taryn's screen for a long time, then shook his head. "Have you answered them yet?"

"Not yet."

Suddenly Doug grabbed at his head with both hands, his face squeezed into a grimace of surprise and pain.

"What is it?" Miranda asked.

Before he could answer, Taryn jerked in her chair and put her hands over her ears. Seconds later, Miranda gasped as a roar filled her head, erasing not only all other sound but all shreds of rational thought.

176

AS THE WORDS MARCHED ACROSS his screen, Elijah covered his ears and closed his eyes, hoping to shut out the roar that seemed about to burst his skull. It was a mistake. Now, as the roar grew in intensity, images filled the screen of his mind, images more vivid than normal sight, unfolding with infinite clarity. A plate-glass store window shattered outward in a blast of flame and smoke. On the sidewalk a man in a blue-and-white seersucker suit was flung to the ground, the suit reddening as he went down; a woman fell, one hand clutching her throat, blood pouring down her face. Her shopping bag arced across the gleaming black hood of a car parked at the curb, turning in slow motion as blue-and-purple tissue paper and white boxes cascaded onto the cobblestone street.

Elijah clutched the arms of his chair and opened his eyes to force away the images. He focused on his marble, which was sitting on the desk, next to his keyboard. But through the clear glass he saw, instead of the familiar swirl of blue and white, the orange of flames. A voice cut through the roar in his head, and he could not tell if it was his own voice or another's. *"The lake! Go to the lake!"*

He closed his eyes again, willing himself to fill his mind with an image of the lake. Its surface was churned by wind and wave into a maelstrom of roiling water. He imagined himself standing at the edge of the dock, wind and spray in his face, and then flinging himself headfirst into the water, breaking through the froth and confusion, angling downward through powerful currents that pushed him one way and another. He stroked down and down until he reached the cool green stillness near the bottom. *Breathe.*

177

He took a long, shuddering breath and another, as if he could breathe in water instead of air. His heart slowed, and he became aware that the roaring had quieted. Flickers of sunlight wavered through the green depths and marked the rippled sand beneath him. *Stillness.* He did not hear the word so much as he felt it move slowly through his body. *When you go deep enough there is always stillness.*

August 1, 2000—11:19 A.M. _____

DOUG OPENED HIS EYES AND gave his head a shake. The roar had quit, replaced with a sense of quiet and calm as inexplicable as the roar had been. He rubbed his forehead between his eyes, where a headache had begun. Next to him, Miranda was blinking as if waking from a dream, her face as perplexed as he knew his own must be. Whatever had just happened, it had happened to her, too. Taryn sat very still, her thin fingers interlaced in her lap, her eyes closed.

He turned to check on Elijah. The boy was so still he might have been carved of dark granite, his hands on the arms of his chair, his head bowed. Doug could not see his chest move as he breathed. He went to him and put his hands on the boy's shoulders. "Elijah," he said, shaking him gently, as if to wake him up. Elijah didn't stir. Doug looked at the computer screen.

Path:
Laurel.grt.com!news.amherst.edu!news.mtholyoke.edu!lll-winkenlln1.-gov!agate!bass!clarinews

178

From: clarinews@clarinet.com (AP)
Message-ID: <crew-riotUR457_3b8@clarinet.com>
Date: Mon, 31 Jul 00 22:35:40EDT

> GREENWICH, CT (AP)—Fifty-three people are dead and scores injured
> or unaccounted for in an unprecedented eruption of violence in
> this affluent suburban community. Two homemade bombs went off in
> an upscale shopping mall at 4:30 this afternoon, killing and
> wounding shoppers and pedestrians and setting fire to two
> buildings. As stunned survivors went to the aid of the wounded
> and dying, a group of young men later identified as members of
> Apocalypse, one of New York City's most vicious crews, emerged
> from a black-painted school bus and opened fire with
> semiautomatic weapons. A gun battle with arriving police
> officers resulted in the deaths of five crew members, a
> bystander, and one policeman.
>   "It's like war," Police Chief Martin Elsen said. "There was no
> intention here except to kill." Racial motivation has been ruled
> out; Apocalypse is one of the few mixed-race crews in the
> country. A phone caller to police headquarters took credit for
> the attack in the name of the United Front for Economic
> Equalization.
>   According to the FBI, this may be the first wave of a planned
> assault on affluent communities across the country. An informed
> source says that UFEE is organizing inner-city gangs and the
> hard-core unemployed for an all-out war against the rich. "Class
> warfare," the source called it. "If I was rich, I would no longer
> feel safe in America."

179

Tuesday, 8/1
Patient #4978 / Taryn Forrester

"The mysterious...is the source of all true art and science."
—Albert Einstein

Copernicus. Galileo. Newton. Einstein. All paradigm shifters.

Such men must be willing to consider the mysterious—the apparently impossible.

POSSIBLE	IMPOSSIBLE
1. Fantasy-prone/schizophrenic (as diagnosed)	1. Extreme psychic abilities
2. "Church of St. Taryn" a con game	2. Child actually performed "miracles"!
3. Mother's reports of child's abilities delusional	3. Mother's reports accurate
4. Marian's observation a coincidence	4. Child "reads" with her hands
5. Birds dive-bombing Randolph a natural occurrence	5. Child "called" them
6. Child fantasizes animal deaths	6. Clairvoyance
7. Child pretended an answer from Detroit	7. Remote telepathy

Paradigm shift?

"Drummed out of the APA," Abigail said. Could the actual purpose of the GFGHP be to conduct research on this patient's psychic powers? Choosing Miranda Ellenby could have been a diversion to keep me from suspecting the true nature of their work.

If a paradigm shift is to come from research at Laurel Mountain, it will not come from the Periodeses!

180

THE SOUND OF HER RUNNING *feet against the floor does not shut out the sounds behind her, the rhythmic thumps, the thunderous growl. Miranda snatches at the door, jerks it open, plunges down the narrow basement steps. She hears the heavy feet stop, senses the lion hesitating at the stairs. Her heart leaps. Maybe there will be time to close herself into the laundry room. But at the bottom of the steps she freezes. There is no laundry room, only blank stone walls, and the lion is coming now, his huge body moving slowly but steadily downward. She scrabbles at the farthest wall, desperate for a way through. Nothing.*

She turns. The lion, purple and massive, faces her. Teeth gleam above a lolling purple tongue.

There is nothing to lose, Miranda thinks. He'll get me anyway. Her back pressed to the hard stone of the wall behind her, she reaches a shaking hand out toward the beast. "Easy, boy," she says. "Easy. Come here." The lion crouches to spring.

And Miranda was awake, staring into the darkness, her heart thudding against her ribs. That's how the nightmare finally stopped! She hadn't tied the lion up or chained it down. She had tamed it.

She lay there, listening to the wind in the trees outside her window, letting herself calm down as the dream faded. Breathing. Thinking.

What had happened on the lawn on Sunday when the four of them had connected? When Timmy had raised the rock, she had been focused on the image in front of her eyes—boy, rock, arms moving, and Jemma sitting on the grass, unaware. She remembered the horror that had filled her, the energy surging between them, and herself thinking, *No! Nothing more than that, just No!*

What if, instead, she had closed her eyes and used her mind to make an image not of Timmy but of his intention? As if it were a live thing, as if it were a lion charging—not at Jemma but at her. And what if she had done what she had done in her old nightmare? Reached out to it, petted it, hugged it, scratched behind its ears, talking to it all the while. What if, connected, as the energy surged between them, all four of them had done that?

August 2, 2000—1:30 P.M._____

"No," DOUG SAID, HIS BACK to the swirling fractal images of his screen saver. His face was set, his eyes intense. "Suppose this visualization you're suggesting really works? You don't reach out to a lion that's coming to kill you!"

"Why not? There was no way out, nowhere to go. It would have gotten me anyway. Isn't it like that in the world? There's no place safe. There's nothing to lose."

"There's always something to lose!"

Taryn swiveled back and forth in her chair. "We can't just do what we did before. If we reflect violence someone gets hurt. *We* hurt someone."

Elijah, sitting on the floor between Doug and Taryn, nodded.

"And we can't skip it off like a stone, because no matter where it went it would still be violence. It could still hurt someone. But if we tamed it—"

182

"It wouldn't be violence anymore," Miranda finished. Her face was radiant with the possibility. "That bit of violence would be gone from the world!"

"Whatever this is we have, it's not about Timmy Lasko with a rock!" Doug waved his hand toward the basket of Elijah's print-outs. "*That's* violence, and it isn't just some mental image. It isn't a dream. It's real. People are dying. Nobody could 'tame' what's happening out there. Reach out to that, and you'll get swallowed up!"

August 3, 2000—2:03 A.M. _____

TARYN SAT LOOKING OUT HER window into the moon-splashed darkness under the trees, stroking the furry leaves of the violet with one finger. The house around her was hushed. She could feel the even breathing as the others slept. There was nothing stirring outside. No wind. The trees were silent. There was no shadow where a shadow shouldn't be. So why was she afraid?

The violet's delicate flowers made lighter spots against the background of dark leaves. She touched one gently and shivered. Silence here, too. Silence everywhere.

August 3, 2000—4:52 A.M. _____

DOUG RISES IN HIS STIRRUPS to ease his back, flexes his hands in his gloves. The fire behind them is close enough now to light their way with a ruddy glow; explosions shake the ground beneath the

183

horses' hooves. Still the peaks of the mountains rise in the distance, taller but scarcely closer.

Next to him the black horse keeps pace with his own, its rider little more than a red-tinged shadow in the gloom. The cat is a pale shape that turns to him now, green irises glowing. There is no cover ahead, nothing to break the smooth line of the waving grass that stirs in the wind. No cover and no path.

An explosion erupts behind him, kicking up clots of dirt that spatter against his back. He tightens his grip on the reins as his horse stumbles. Another explosion rips through the darkness, lighting the sky as his horse goes down, flinging Doug from the saddle into a swirl of black smoke.

August 3, 2000—1:15 P.M._____

MIRANDA WHAPPED THE TETHERBALL AND watched Doug, unsmiling, duck as it flew past his head. It was a glorious day, the sort of day that made even the patients at Laurel Mountain want to stay outdoors. Clear, sunny, dry, and cool. The lake sparkled, and the smell of balsam and pine filled the air. Polly Perky had organized the older children from the lodge into games on the lawn, and there was a festive atmosphere to the usual organized chaos. The Ark family had eaten a picnic lunch and agreed not to go back into the computer lab afterward. But Doug had seemed distracted during lunch. Distant. Miranda had challenged him to this game, hoping to have a time alone, away from the others. Noah had taken the lunch things inside, Taryn and Elijah were playing checkers on a quilt near the path to the house, and Abigail, doing

184

her needlepoint, sat on a bench nearby. The tetherball pole was far enough away to let the two of them talk as they played without being overheard. But Doug wasn't talking. Miranda felt his distance like an empty space in the center of herself.

When the ball came around again, he swung at it and missed.

"You aren't paying the slightest attention," she told him.

Frowning at something over her shoulder, he seemed not to have heard her. She turned. Turnbull, in a light summer suit, his tie loosened, was strolling down from the lodge. Turning back, she hit the ball again. As she watched it circle the pole, she was aware that Turnbull was passing them, moving toward where Taryn and Elijah were sitting with the checkerboard. He moved into her line of vision, still strolling casually, and stopped beside a tree near the quilt. He leaned against the trunk, his body angled toward a croquet game Pew was supervising among four girls, as if to watch.

Doug slammed the ball as it came around, sending it careening upward on its rope. "Spying," he said.

Miranda let the ball wind around the pole once before hitting it back. "Who's he spying on?"

"Taryn! Just watch his eyes. Noah and Abigail ought to take the note I found in his computer files seriously. Paradigm shift!" Doug smashed the ball with his fist, and it wound itself around the pole.

"Your point. One to nothing." She unwound the ball from the pole. "They say there's nothing he can do."

"They underestimate him." Doug hit the ball well over her head. "I've been reading his files. Patients aren't people to him. They're lab animals. And Laurel Mountain isn't a hospital for sick kids, it's a place to make a name for himself. Any way he can."

Miranda cocked her arm to hit the ball as it slowed, but suddenly her head was filled with a loud growling sound. She looked around her for the source of the sound, then understood it was not coming from outside. Doug had turned toward the croquet game. She saw what he was looking at, and the sound of it rose above the noise in her head. Hannah, one of the croquet players, had smacked Florence's ball out of play, and Florence was brandishing her croquet mallet, threatening at the top of her lungs to knock Hannah's head across the lake. Pew had managed to get herself between the two, but she was too busy avoiding the business end of the swinging mallet to make a serious effort to take it away.

The lion! Miranda saw Taryn reach for Elijah's hand. She grabbed Doug's and pulled him toward the others. *See the lion!* Miranda sank to her knees on the quilt and reached for the hand Taryn was holding out to her. Her fingers tightened around Doug's as she felt him pull back, remain standing.

Time slowed. Moments separated themselves into still pictures. Pew's hands up. The mallet swinging back in jerky stop-start moves. Florence's face twisted in a grimace of fury. Pew's hands stretching forward.

Miranda closed her eyes. Awareness flowed into her, intensifying as she imagined with the clarity of a dream the movement of the lion charging, teeth bared, saliva dripping. It came thundering toward her and leapt, its huge paws, claws out, striking her in the chest. She felt herself thrown back by the impact, the pain of claws ripping flesh so intense, so surprising, she nearly pulled away, nearly broke contact.

With an effort, she forced herself to remember what she needed to do, forced her arms forward, flinging them around the

186

lion's neck. *Easy, boy, easy.* She hugged it to her, ruffling its mane, pushing her fingers through the thick hair to rub behind its tawny ears. And felt the animal still. Felt it settle slowly back onto its haunches. *Easy, boy. It's okay.* She put her cheek against its muzzle. *Easy now.*

Suddenly, it snarled and pulled its head back, its rank breath hot on her face. She struggled to keep her arms around its neck, but it roared, raising a paw that ripped at her arm. It broke free, then turned to launch itself with a roar into another charge, away from where she sprawled, stunned with pain.

When the lion struck his chest, Doug fought the pain, jerked his hand free, and opened his eyes, focusing on where Harlan Turnbull had stepped away from the tree, toward the commotion. Everything he had read in the man's files flooded back to him, and he concentrated his rage. *There! Get him! Take him down!* Doug heard the snarl, the roar. He closed his eyes and saw the lion turn, wheeling on its back legs, to charge the figure in blue and white. He made the image as vivid as he could, then watched the lion, claws tearing, bring the figure down.

Harlan Turnbull sat up, blinking, a pale blue bruise already swelling on his forehead where the mallet had struck him when Florence swung and let it go. Florence, a bewildered look on her face, began to cry.

Pew hurried forward to help Turnbull to his feet.

"I never meant to." Florence wailed, crumpling to the ground. "I never meant to throw it. You gotta believe me! I meant to hit Hannah with it, not him. I did!"

Elijah, Taryn, and Miranda dropped hands, sitting in stunned and unmoving silence as the noise and movement flowed around them. Doug, knees shaking, sank to the grass.

Leaning on Pew, Turnbull stared past Florence at Taryn, his face contorted with fury. Then he brushed Pew away and refused Abigail's offer to help him to the infirmary. He looked at Taryn again, his pale eyes cold, then turned, holding his head, and walked unsteadily back toward the lodge.

August 3, 2000—1:40 P.M._____

WHEN AT LAST THEY HAD THE energy to move, they had stumbled back to the house, Abigail fussing over them uncertainly.

"You did that! You sent the lion after Turnbull." Taryn glared at Doug.

Doug looked up, his eyes defiant in a haggard face. "I had to know if it could work."

Taryn wrapped her arms around her knees and put her head down on them, her hair making a dark curtain around her face.

Elijah spoke, his voice low and soft. "Mama Effie said there's nothing so good it can't be used for evil."

Doug picked up a pencil from the coffee table and began weaving it through his fingers.

"You said violence was real," Taryn said to Doug. "Well, so is this power. As real as the mountain or the trees out there. If we use it to add to the violence—"

"We make everything worse," Miranda finished.

"We were taming the lion," Taryn said. "If you had worked

188

with us, we could have taken that one tiny bit of violence out of the world!"

Doug broke the pencil between his fingers. "Turnbull's dangerous! We can't just let people like that..." His voice dwindled and stopped. He looked at Taryn.

The image of a deer, headless in the snow, filled her mind and his. "You can't do it their way," she said. "You aren't one of them. You never were."

Thursday, 8/3
Patient #4978 / Taryn Forrester

There is more to this child's abilities than telepathy and clairvoyance!

PK. Psychokinesis. The ability to move objects with the power of the mind.

There is no other explanation for the direction and trajectory of the croquet mallet that struck me. This is no interesting mental anomaly—PK used the way this child can use it is *dangerous*. And she has clearly targeted me!

Journal—Miranda Ellenby
August 4, 2000—1:45 P.M.

Fog is swirling around outside and pressing against the window like millions of ghosts trying to get in. Can't see the lake or even the nearest trees. It gives me the shivers.

    Today is the first day since we all came to the Ark that someone besides "family" is in the house—aside from the time Turnbull brought the president of the board to spy on us. Pew (whose name is really Mary Alice) is baby-sitting Taryn and me. Not that we need a baby-sitter, but there's a rule. Laurel Mountain patients aren't allowed to be left unsupervised, even for an hour, let alone an afternoon. And without Pew, we'd be alone. Abigail's up at the lodge, having sessions with some of her other patients and the guys are out on the mountain somewhere.

    They'd been planning a "Men's Day Out" hike for ages, and in spite of Abigail's protests, they went ahead with it. Noah pulled a big macho routine about how a little fog and rain weren't going to deter real men. But I think he mainly wanted to go ahead with business as usual to show us all that he isn't spooked by Turnbull. Besides, Doug had already programmed the boundary alarms by the lake trail to shut down. So they put ponchos on over their backpacks and went off into the woods, disappearing like firemen into heavy smoke.

    I don't know what's going on with Doug. He hasn't been talking, not even online. It's like he's been pulling against the connections. What he did to Turnbull yesterday scares me, and

191

I keep remembering tire irons and hunting knives.

But I was outside when they were leaving this morning, and he let Noah and Elijah start without him. When we were alone on the porch he grabbed my hand. He didn't say anything, he just squeezed it. Like he was testing to see if I was real. The look he gave me went straight through me—and it wasn't my head responding! My knees got all rubbery. I squeezed back. Then he just jumped down the steps and ran to catch up to the others. Didn't turn and wave or anything, just vanished into the fog. It made me wish I was going with them instead of staying here.

He's so paranoid about Turnbull that last night he went around the whole Ark looking for bugs—microphone bugs. Noah said there was no way Turnbull could have planted any, but I keep remembering when I was changing on Visitors' Day and Turnbull was heading up here—he had to know Noah and Abigail were out on the lawn, and he didn't know I was here. He thought he was coming to an empty house. What for?

Doug didn't find any microphones. But just the idea of Turnbull bugging the house made me paranoid, too. If it was anybody but Pew in the lab with Taryn right now, I'd suspect Turnbull had sent a spy. But not Pew. She may not have much head, but she's got plenty of heart, and there's no way she'd side with Turnbull against a kid. No way. Besides, we chose her, Turnbull didn't.

Taryn's giving her a computer lesson now, and I told her I'd help her with French later. I have to be able to improve on that accent! When I left the lab they'd found a bunch of candid photos of movie stars that rabid fans put on the nets, and Pew was having a great time, thinking computers were maybe worth something after all.

I couldn't stay there. Maybe it's because there aren't any windows, but I got too jittery. I felt cut off. I don't like having the guys off someplace where we can't reach them. I don't even like having Abigail up at the lodge. It makes me want to put double locks on all the doors. Not that this window makes much difference in the fog. Can't see anything, anyway.

Sound gets strange when it's wet out—it carries differently. There was a woodpecker pounding out in the woods somewhere a few minutes ago—a deep, hollow thumping that seemed to echo, so it was hard to tell where it was coming from or how far away.

And then just a minute ago, there were a couple of thumps that could have been somebody on the porch or could have been from clear up at the lodge. I stopped typing to listen, but I didn't hear anything more. For once writing in my journal is probably hurting more than it's helping. The more I write the more

August 4, 2000—2:01 P.M._____

MIRANDA'S HANDS FROZE AS A SCREAM reverberated through the house. *Taryn!* She pushed back her chair and had begun to get up when the room began to spin. She sank back into her chair, fear washing over her. An image centered itself in her mind—Turnbull's face, flushed, damp, shiny. A sharp, burning pain

193

knifed through her consciousness. *Taryn!* She clutched at the name, a point of focus, as she felt her mind slip sideways, a sickening sensation, replaced almost immediately by nothingness. Darkness. Silence.

Miranda blinked once. Twice. And forced herself to see what was in front of her—the computer screen, white letters on blue, the knotty-pine wall of her room behind, fog against the window. Her room. What had happened? Then her mind seemed to snap on. *Taryn!* She flung herself from her chair and hurried down the hall.

The door of the lab was open; no one was inside. On the monitor where Taryn and Pew had been working a photo of a woman in a low-cut red dress gleamed. *Not long enough for the screen saver to come on,* the thought registered as Miranda headed for the living room.

Pew, wringing her hands, stood just inside the room. Behind her stood Turnbull, in his white coat. "Go!" he said over his shoulder, gesturing toward the door with one hand. In the other he held an empty syringe and needle. Beyond Turnbull Miranda saw one of the male psychiatric nurses, carrying Taryn, back his way through the screen door and out into the fog. Taryn's thin arms and legs dangled and her head, eyes closed, lolled against the man's chest.

"...medical director," Turnbull was saying to Pew. "The welfare of each patient is my responsibility." He turned to Miranda. "This has nothing to do with you."

Before Miranda could think what to do or say, Turnbull bent toward the coffee table and scooped up the audiotapes stacked next to the tape recorder. "No!" she said. He looked at her, his lips compressed into a tight, thin line. Deliberately, he popped open the recorder and took the tape that was inside.

"Hospital property," he said as he pocketed the tapes and followed the nurse out the front door.

Pew turned to Miranda, tears spilling over. "What could I do?" she wailed. "He's the boss!"

August 4, 2000—4:20 P.M. _____

"HE STARTED THAT KEENING SOUND and then just collapsed on the trail and went quiet," Noah told Abigail and Miranda when he'd removed Elijah's wet pack and poncho. The boy was huddled near the fire Abigail had started to ward off the damp chill. "We'd have been back sooner, but we couldn't get him up at first. He just sat there in the mud, rocking. I thought we might have to carry him back, but Doug finally got through to him."

"We both felt it," Doug said. "I didn't know what it was, only that something had happened to Taryn. I told him we couldn't do anything about it out there on the mountain." He sat down next to Elijah and touched his shoulder. Elijah, his arms around his legs, his head down, began rocking.

"We came as fast as we could." Noah gathered the dripping ponchos and dropped them outside on the porch. "I should have listened to you and postponed the hike. I never should have left!"

Abigail, slumped in the rocker, shook her head. "Who would have thought the man would do such a thing! He knows he has no authorization. When Miranda and Mary Alice came to get me, I couldn't believe it."

"He can't keep her, can he?" Doug asked. "He can't just take her and keep her."

"The psychological argument failed, so I'd be willing to bet he'll claim some kind of medical emergency." Noah sank onto the couch. "Plague, no doubt, or typhoid! I should have remembered he had a trump card. We aren't M.D.s—it won't be easy to beat him on this one."

Abigail sighed. "We can't very well insist the medical director get a second opinion."

Miranda tried to still her thoughts, to force a calm space inside where she could get a sense of Taryn, that wisp of living presence that had grown so slowly she had come to take it for granted even before she had understood what it was. But there was only blankness now, the blankness that had been with her since that sickening lurch the moment before her mind went dark. She looked at Doug and Elijah and felt the blankness moving between them.

"We'll fight this, though," Noah said. "We'll figure a way to get her back."

Abigail set her chair rocking in rhythm with Elijah's movement. The orange glow of the firelight flickered over them. "It'll be okay," she said, her voice more determined than sure. "We're a family. Families are forever."

August 5, 2000—5:30 A.M. _____

LIKE AN EXHAUSTED DIVER, Taryn struggled up through darkness toward a distant light, trying to hold on to memory that seemed

196

to weigh her down, pull her back. When she opened her eyes she could not make sense of the dimly lit room, the colors and shapes. *Not right,* she thought, but could not finish the effort, could not explain to herself what was wrong. Images were blurred, grayed, as if she lay behind smoky glass. She blinked. Nothing changed.

She tried to remember where she was, how she had come to be here. Images swirled—a face, too close; a hand on her wrist; another, hurting; a needle; darkness.

She lay still, listening. Silence. She closed her eyes again and must have slept. When next she looked sunlight knifed downward through the window onto the gray-green blanket humped over her feet. The blanket looked familiar but wrong. Her mind refused to focus. She turned her head, looked at the closed door, its oblong window catching the light. The lodge, she thought then, relieved at the sudden flash of understanding. They've brought me to the lodge. Relief faded as she lay there trying to sense beyond the flat, blank surface of the door the energy—confusion, sadness, anger— that had always pulsed around her in this place. Nothing.

She looked out the window toward the deep green tops of the pines and tried to let herself feel their living presence. Nothing.

Fear washed over her. She felt bound, blindfolded, muffled. She tried to shake herself awake, free herself from whatever held her. And could not. There was nothing except the room, except a scattering of disjointed sounds beyond.

She could remember the faces, the hands, the needle. Forcing herself to concentrate, she remembered other images that had swum above her as she lay in this bed on her back. Thin blond hair above a bland pink face. The face smiling. Smiling and say-ing words she could hardly hear, that seemed to have no meaning.

Another needle. *Turnbull*—the name came to her with a twinge to her stomach.

Drugs. It felt as if her mind were being chopped apart, connections severed. The self she knew was trapped in a tiny dark space with fewer and fewer pathways to the world. Only a trickle of sound, of sight came through. And nothing else. Nothing else.

What day is it? What time? She could not answer.

Taryn blinked again. The room was flat, like a photo, a pattern without depth. She slowed her breath, focused inside, reached into her body, feeling the covers against her skin, the hair on her forehead, the pressure of the pillow beneath her head.

Then, with all her strength, she reached—toward the Ark, toward Miranda, Elijah, Doug. Nothing. She felt like a runner fighting a hurricane, forced to her knees, forced, at last, to turn for shelter. She took a long, deep breath and closed her eyes, tears warm against her cheeks. How long would it take, she wondered, for the pathways to be cut forever, leaving her a prisoner inside her skin?

To: Harlan Turnbull, M.D., Ph.D.
FROM: Noah Periodes, Ph.D.
DATE: August 5, 2000
RE: Taryn Forrester, Patient #4978
COPY: Harold Deitz

Please keep Abigail and me informed of Taryn's progress on a daily basis.

I'd be interested in knowing, Harlan, how you were able to diagnose a bacterial infection at 2 P.M. on Friday that had not shown itself through any recognizable symptoms before Abigail left at 12:45 to meet with another patient at the lodge. For that matter, we've wondered how you suspected illness in the first place without direct contact with the patient.

Please send copies of the lab reports on the bacteria. The other members of our therapeutic family have all been exposed and we would like to know what we've been exposed to.

And finally, the audiotapes of the GFGHP meetings are the sole property of this research project. We expect their immediate return!

HARLAN TURNBULL, M.D., PH.D. — NOTES

Saturday, 8/5
GFGHP TAPES

Incredible!

Have copied and listened to the tapes. The Periodeses seem
to have stumbled onto dynamite. Or maybe pure gold. Mind
energy. What's happening with these children could be
worth a fortune, depending on what can be done with it.
How it can be controlled.

Mental connections around the world!
Shared dreaming!
Group psychokinesis!

Deitz has accepted medical authority for removing the
Forrester child. But there's little point having her alone
(though she is clearly the most adept) when the phenomenon
affects all four. How to get control of the others? And
how to protect against the use of their power while
studying it?

Must consider what Deitz will buy into. Paradigm shift.
New science. Psychology for the new century. A way to put
Laurel Mountain on the map.

We hope she'll be well and back on the nets by the end
of the week, but we can't be sure. She'll send you a msg.
as soon as she can.

Miranda finished the message and sent it off to all the children
Taryn had been interacting with. She stretched and rubbed at the
back of her neck. By the end of the week, she had said. Almost
certainly a lie.

"It's my fault!"

Miranda jumped. She hadn't heard Doug come into the lab.
She swiveled around to look at him. His eyes were clouded, and
his face looked closed down. "She said he was afraid of her. He
must have blamed her for the croquet mallet. If I hadn't sent the
lion to attack, he wouldn't have taken her."

Miranda shrugged. "You don't know that."

"Have you seen what Elijah found this morning?" Doug took
the top sheet out of Elijah's box. "German police found a cache of
smuggled plutonium and thought they'd solved a major mystery—
except that what they found turned out to be less than half of
what was stolen. The group that stole it have already threatened
to nuke a major city, just to show they can do it. The police say
it's only a matter of time."

Miranda shivered. "I don't want to hear it. Where is Elijah?"

"I left him with Abigail. Rocking and spinning his marble.
He's been like my shadow since Turnbull snatched Taryn, and he
hasn't said word one. Noah let him go up to the lodge lab with me
today because I had some work to do up there. I showed him how

to get into the main memory to keep him off the news nets." Doug threw the paper back into the box. "This last piece is just about all I can take."

Miranda felt tiredness wash over her and longed to go to bed and pull the covers over her head. "I can't seem to make the reaching work anymore. It's like I'm running on half power without Taryn. Everything's harder, darker, scarier."

Doug nodded. "I keep thinking about negative intentions making the lion stronger...."

Miranda reached to touch his hand. She had wanted their connection back when he had pulled away. Now she almost wished it away again. "Don't think about it. What's done is done."

"While I was at the lodge I broke into Turnbull's files to plant a virus—wipe out all his files. Everything. Personal documents, research records, everything."

"You didn't—"

"I didn't. I just sat there, looking at his directories, drawer after drawer of files, thinking about what he's doing to Taryn. Feeling the emptiness where she used to be, like a hole in my mind—in myself. Wondering if what he's doing to her is what he did to Gordon Stephenson—if she'll ever be able to come back from it. I was so angry it was like plugging into a huge generator. Like the way I felt the night with the tire iron. I wanted to smash everything Turnbull stands for and then go after him."

"And?"

"And I couldn't. If Taryn's right, it has to change everything, doesn't it? No matter what he does, how can we fight him if fighting makes him stronger? Makes the world darker? It's too dark as it is!"

202

Miranda listened to the hum of the computers, wondering how anyone could fight without fighting.

"Do you belong to a church?"

Miranda looked up at Doug in surprise. "Church? No. We used to go on Christmas Eve, but that's all. Why?"

"I do. Did. My family's CHRISTIAN. You know, in all caps. Taking Jesus as our personal savior and all that. Only nobody seemed to hear what Jesus really said. *Turn the other cheek. Love your enemies.* The people at our church skipped that part—or else they jumped back to the Old Testament when it came to enemies. Eye for an eye; tooth for a tooth. What they were, what they wanted to be, was Christian soldiers!

"The thing is, if Jesus was right, my family and my church had it all wrong. And if he was wrong, he not only wasn't God; he was a wimp. He let them kill him without even trying to fight back. Either way—" Doug leaned against a filing cabinet.

"My father says religions are a great excuse to go to war," Miranda said.

"That's what's so weird. Jesus wasn't the only one who told people not to slaughter each other. The message has been coming into the world over and over again. People don't listen, but the message is there. There's no such thing as a holy war! What Taryn said about the lion is just another way to say the same thing. You can't fight negative energy with more negative energy, violence with more violence. I want to fight Turnbull to get Taryn back, but how could we, even if we knew how? If he keeps her..." Doug's voice trailed off.

With a barely audible snap Miranda's screen saver came on, spangling her monitor with colors. She watched the liquid move-

203

ment spiraling designs where moments ago there were the words she had written. "Chaos patterns," she said. "Isn't that what fractals are? Patterns out of the patternless? Designs where you can't see designs? Maybe till Taryn comes back we go into screen-saver mode. Just shut down."

"And what if he doesn't let her come back?"

August 7, 2000—2:30 P.M._____

HAROLD DEITZ BEGAN GATHERING PAPERS to put into his briefcase. "I'm pleased at your success getting Randolph to fund a protocol. Research the foundation doesn't have to pay for is welcome, whatever the project. By the way, you said you'd put the Forrester girl in isolation, but you didn't say why. What does she have?"

Harlan Turnbull turned from the coffee machine near the window, the pot in his hand. "It seems to be a drug-resistant bacteria. Highly contagious."

"Well, don't take any chances. We don't need an epidemic like the flu of '98—what a disaster that was!" He snapped his briefcase shut. "So. Anything else?"

"There is something." Turnbull held up the coffeepot. "Would you like another cup?"

Deitz shook his head.

Turnbull filled his own mug and brought it to the table. He sat down, moved his own pile of papers out of the way, and sipped his coffee. "As you know, I have a personal commitment to putting Laurel Mountain on the psychological map, so to speak. And I've always believed that research, provided it's bold and

204

challenging—even paradigm shifting—will accomplish that goal."

"Do you have a new project in mind?"

Turnbull set down his mug. "This is more in the nature of a philosophical suggestion. Our focus, naturally enough, has been the *problems* of the mind. But what about the other side of the coin? What about the *powers* of the mind?"

"Powers?"

"Consider autistic savants. In spite of their terrible—crippling—mental deficits, they have astonishing abilities."

"Such as?"

"Some savants can tell you what day of the week a date will fall on in any year, past or future. Some can beat calculators at math computations. There are art savants, music savants, even geographical savants. According to what we think we know about the mind, their abilities seem virtually impossible—playing a whole symphony after a single hearing, for instance. And yet there they are. Research on savant abilities might give us a whole new perspective on the latent capacities of the human mind."

"We don't have a savant at Laurel Mountain, do we?"

Turnbull shrugged. "It's possible that Elijah Raymond is one. But savant abilities aren't the only examples of unusual powers of the mind that might be investigated by an institution on the cutting edge of psychological research. Have you ever heard of psychokinesis?"

"Isn't that extreme hyperactivity?"

"That's the psychiatric term. But there's another meaning—the use of mental energy to move physical objects."

Deitz sniffed. "You mean like that Israeli con man? The one who used to say he could bend spoons with his mind?"

205

"Not exactly." Turnbull sipped his coffee. "Physicists have done research proving that people can use their minds to influence a random-number generator, for instance. That's one kind of psychokinesis. The research is impeccable."

Deitz sat up and took the handle of his briefcase, as if preparing to leave. "Physicists? Random-number generators? I can't see that sort of research having anything to do with Laurel Mountain."

"I offer it only as an example of well-documented psychokinesis." Turnbull cleared his throat. "I was trying to suggest that there are lines of research we haven't previously considered that might bring a good deal of attention to our work. Savant abilities, psychokinesis, precognitive dreams, clairvoyance, telepathy—"

"Clairvoyance? Telepathy?" Deitz snorted. "That would bring attention to our work all right!" He stood up. "Gypsies and mad Russians! If word got out that we were 'researching' that sort of thing we'd be out of business in a week. Can you imagine parents trusting their children to a collection of crackpots who study tarot cards and mind reading?"

"I didn't mean to suggest—"

"I should hope not! Listen, Harlan, if you or the Periodeses want to devise some research on that autistic boy's savant abilities, go right ahead. Write it up. Make a proposal. But for heaven's sake, don't bring those other things into it." He shuddered. "Don't even use the words."

He went to the door and turned back, one hand on the knob. "I tell you the truth, Harlan—if we thought for one moment anyone here was conducting that sort of research the foundation would shut the place down. I mean it. Cut the funding off cold and shut it down. I'd be the first to insist on it. There is no way I would allow my name or the name of the foundation to be associated with that kind of parapsychological mumbo jumbo."

From the Desk of
HARLAN TURNBULL, M.D., Ph.D.

To: Noah Periodes
From: HT
Re: GFGHP Tapes
Date: August 8, 2000

Herewith I am returning the tapes of your official
"family meetings." I disagree with your assessment
of the ownership issue, but you are welcome to
retain the originals. I have made copies for my own
files and mailed others to Harold Deitz. When he has
read my cover letter and listened to the tapes, I
feel certain that he will withdraw his support for
the GFGHP project (along with that of the
foundation). Harold Deitz has no tolerance for
what he terms "parapsychological mumbo jumbo."

ABIGAIL CARRIED ELIJAH INTO HIS room and settled him onto his bed. He had sat in the corner of the couch since they came in from swimming, until he'd finally rocked himself to sleep. She pulled his coverlet over him and ran a hand over his hair. His face had settled into the smooth softness of a little boy's, the lines of waking pain erased in sleep. But even in sleep his right hand stayed clenched around his marble.

All three of them had changed since Taryn had been taken, their energies diminished. Elijah, though, had been most affected. He seemed to have been thrust back into his shell, as if Taryn's disappearance had been another in the catalog of deaths in his short life.

Abigail fought down the pain that rose at the thought of Taryn, drugged and out of reach. And Turnbull's memo. Like a hole chopped in the bottom of the Ark. "Family is forever." How long had she known that she must not make such promises to children? And yet she'd said it. Worse, she had dared to believe it.

Noah had left for Lake Placid as soon as they'd read the memo, knowing he would get to Deitz before the tapes, hoping against hope to remake the old case for the Ark. Therapeutic family. Not a breath of parapsychological mumbo jumbo. He had taken Taryn's poetry, bolstered himself with the miracle of Elijah beginning to talk. A therapeutic family that was undeniably helping children. Hoping it would be enough to offset the tapes when they came.

It wouldn't work, Abigail knew. Deitz would hear their voices admitting belief in powers that couldn't, in Deitz's version of reality, exist.

"Seeing isn't believing," she had said as Noah struggled with his tie, pulled on his jacket, searched for his car keys. "It's the other way around. What Deitz believes is all he can see. We knew this was dangerous stuff."

Noah had had to go, anyway. Had to try. Abigail sighed, then tucked the coverlet more snugly under Elijah's chin.

August 8, 2000—4:05 P.M. _____

ELIJAH PEERS BENEATH HIM THROUGH *the thickening haze and smoke. He can see only the black horse, its rider uncertain, turning this way and that. Smoke, thick and black and oily, burns his lungs. Wind rushes past Elijah's head, carrying upward a rumble, like thunder, that grows steadily louder and deeper. Other sounds are coming now, the crackling sound of flames, booming guns, screams. Red-orange light rises from the ground over which he flies. And the sound, always the sound.*

Elijah beats his way upward, wings flapping powerfully, up and up and up into the cool, clear air above. Silence and wind. Never has he flown so high, seen the earth beneath so wide, so curved, falling away into blue at all the edges. Below him mountain peaks shoulder up through the layers of cloud and smoke that lie like a floor to the blue sky above.

A floor he cannot see through. He has lost them.

210

He tips and stills his wings, lets himself slip over the edge of the wind that buoys him, circles lower, and begins a long, sloping descent into the roar of the black roiling clouds. Darkness and then the ruddy light of the fires. People scurry below like ants from an overturned nest. Sound beats against his head, heat singes his wings, forcing him upward into the cold, clear wind.

Again and again, where a break appears in the clouds he slips downward, searching. And feels the sound rising, the smoke and heat filling his lungs. Again and again he rises to fly on.

August 9, 2000—8:30 A.M. _____

"HE'S NOT IN HIS ROOM." Miranda, in T-shirt and cutoffs, padded into the kitchen in bare feet. "Maybe he's in the lab."

"No," Doug said. "I just came from there."

"I checked both bathrooms on the way back. He's not there, either."

Abigail set the plates down on the table with a thud. "You don't suppose Harlan—"

"Of course not. No one's been in the house." Noah turned the heat off under a pan full of scrambled eggs. "Elijah can squeeze himself into a corner hardly big enough for a kitten. Before we start imagining things, let's be sure we've looked every place he might be—every closet and cabinet and under the beds. Doug, you check around outside. And don't worry," he said to Abigail, "if he went out, he hasn't gone far, or he'd have tripped the boundary alarms."

211

"I CHECKED THE ALARM PROGRAM," Doug said when they'd gathered again in the living room, "and the whole west section is shut down. Pretty smart. It's the only section that's all woods. There's not even a trail over there, so security doesn't check it all that often. He was in the lab at the lodge with me yesterday morning; that must have been what he was doing."

"We don't know when he left," Abigail said. "It could have been anytime after eleven o'clock last night—"

"Two," Noah said. "I couldn't sleep. He didn't go out before two. But he wouldn't have gone in the dark!"

"Did he take food?" Miranda asked. "Is there anything gone from the kitchen?"

"Nothing," Abigail said when she'd looked. "All that's missing—besides Elijah—are his clothes. He didn't even take his jacket."

"It's hot," Noah said. "He doesn't need it."

"It won't be hot when the sun goes down," Abigail said.

"We'll just have to find him before that. I'll go tell Harlan that he's probably off the grounds. We'll need to call for a search party. Then Doug and I'll cover the ground we hiked the other day. He might go someplace familiar."

"We'll check the other side of the lake," Abigail said, "where we had the picnic."

"He won't be there," Miranda said. "He won't go where he can be found."

"Don't say that!"

Miranda closed her eyes, dizzy for a moment, and held on to

the back of the couch for support. "It's true. I know it. He doesn't mean to be found."

August 9, 2000 _____

Path:
Laurel.grt.com!news.amherst.edu!news.mtholyoke.edu!lll-winkenlln1.gov!agate!bass!clarinews
From: clarinews@clarinet.com (AP)
Message-ID: <militiaUR237_3b6@clarinet.com
Date: Wed, 9 Aug 00 22:35:40EDT

> PLATTSBURGH, NY (AP)—Simultaneous bomb blasts on both sides of
> the U.S./Canadian border this afternoon destroyed two overpasses
> on Interstate 87, popularly known as the Northway. Casualty
> figures are not yet available, due to the enormous amount of
> destruction, but loss of life is expected to be high, as both
> overpasses were clogged with traffic at the time of the blasts.
>   Before the bombings trucks driving at 35 mph in both lanes had
> tied up traffic for half an hour southbound in Quebec and
> northbound in New York, guaranteeing that both overpasses would
> be carrying the maximum number of vehicles. By the time
> law-enforcement agencies arrived at the twin disaster scenes the
> trucks, which witnesses say were unmarked and unlicensed, had
> disappeared.
>   "I've never seen carnage like this," a New York State
> policeman said on the scene, unable to hold back tears. "There's

> nothing left but a twisted mess of steel and concrete and the
> charred remains of vehicles and people. There must have been a
> gasoline tanker on this span when it went down. Something
> exploded besides the bomb."
>   Officials of the Royal Canadian Mounted Police and the New
> York State Police received identical faxes moments after the
> bombing, claiming credit in the name of the Free Mountain
> Militia. Previously dismissed as a small anarchist fringe group,
> the militia may have been growing in recent years, headquartering
> secretly in the Adirondack wilderness of northeastern New York or
> southern Quebec. "They are demanding an end to government control
> of land use," a spokesman from the RCMP said. "They want to
> eliminate all government, all national boundaries, and all
> regulation of private and public land. Essentially, they are
> demanding the dissolution of both the U.S. and Canadian
> governments and threatening continued violence if these ludicrous
> demands are not met."
>   Canadian Premier Martier and President Harris of the United
> States, conferring by phone, have vowed to join forces in an
> investigation that will eliminate the threat of future acts of
> terrorism in what both agree must remain one of the last vestiges
> of open wilderness on the eastern half of the continent.

August 9, 2000—8:00 P.M._____

ELIJAH LOOKED UP INTO THE dense green overhead, the light going
blue around him. He shivered. All day he had walked and
climbed, moving up and away, trying to escape the roar in his

head that had been growing since Taryn disappeared. The roar that this morning had dragged him from his bed, bursting his skull with a pain that had grown beyond bearing. As if the man, multiplied and multiplied again, was smashing bottles, furniture, faces, nearer and nearer.

He had not escaped it, but the pain had lessened as he struggled on, refusing to rest and let it overtake him again. When the pangs in his stomach had made him think of dinner, he had given in, had stopped climbing. He had found the downed tree, its massive trunk slanting across the forest, held above the ground by the branches of other trees where it had been caught in its fall. The base, as thick as he was tall, was sheathed in moss and ferns—green against green. There, near the circle of jagged black roots pulled free of the ground, the space beneath the trunk was just large enough to hold him.

As the light softened to dusk, he had pulled low branches from the smaller firs, piling them on the ground beneath, which was already springy with needles and moss. The branches made a bed, prickly and fragrant, like the one Doug had made near the lake in the dream. When he judged his pile deep enough Elijah gathered ferns to cover the branches. Then he tore off more branches to make a cover against the growing chill, piling them neatly within reach. Samson, hero of Tondishi, would do this, he knew.

Tondishi had been a world of trees and mountains, like this world, like the world he and his mother and Mama Effie had come from. It was right, he knew, to have come back to such a place.

Now he dipped his hand into the water that trickled downward in a narrow cleft in the rocks a few feet from his shelter. He lifted the silvery cold liquid to his lips and drank. A woodpecker drummed in the distance. The only other sounds were the trickling of the water and the whisper of the branches overhead. And the roar that went steadily on and on beneath it all.

Elijah wiped his hands on his jeans. He took off his sneakers and set them neatly, side by side, against the roots of his fallen tree. He ducked into its shelter, then, moving himself one way and then another, settling the branches beneath him. Then he pulled the other branches over himself, one after another, weaving a screen between himself and the failing light beyond.

He pulled his marble from his pocket and held it to his cheek, feeling its smooth curve, imagining the swirl of blue and white it was now too dark to see. Imagining himself high above it, in the cold, clear, silent wind. He took a long, deep breath. He was breaking the connections. No threads would tie him now to the others, pull him back. Elijah breathed into the pungent darkness and felt the mountain beneath him, huge and still and solid. As Taryn had taught him, he brought the mountain into his mind, filling himself with its size and silence. Holding his marble between stony fingers, Elijah let himself slip down into darkness.

August 16, 2000 _____

THE THROB OF HELICOPTER ROTOR blades beat against Miranda's ears, then faded gradually over the treetops. One last pass while the light lasts, they had said. They were not looking for Elijah.

They were looking for signs of the Free Mountain Militia. "We'll keep our eyes peeled for the kid," they'd said on the first day, when one of the army helicopters had landed in the field behind the lodge. But she had seen it in their eyes. They had no energy to invest in an eight-year-old autistic black kid escaped from the loony bin. Not with a threat to the national security on their minds. This was the last use of helicopters in this area even to search for the militia. If they hadn't found signs of them in a week, they didn't expect to find them at all. She didn't think they had expected to find militia headquartered this close to the American bomb site anyway, any more than Miranda had expected them (or the ground-search teams, either) to find Elijah.

"Might as well not have bothered," she whispered, her mouth against the porch rail. Even Doug, inches away, could not have heard her. Yet he looked at her as if he had. Nodded as if he had. She was not the only one who had known from the start a search would turn up nothing.

They were sitting together on the porch steps, Noah and Abigail in the Adirondack chairs behind them. Through the trees the lake looked like melted butter, slick and still under a gold-tinted sky. Doug leaned his arms against his knees, his flute dangling, useless, from his hands. That first night and the next few days he'd played, hoping the music could weave again the connections it had helped to make. Hoping the music, magic, might reach to where Elijah had gone, lure him back again, into the family.

But the sound had floated up through the trees like smoke from a campfire, drifting and disappearing on the wind. Miranda had clung to the notes until the last moment, feeling outward and upward until there was nothing left to feel but the emptiness of loss.

Seven days. Not even Abigail expected anyone to find him now.

Seven days. Miranda could scarcely remember them—long, hot blank spaces between dawn and dusk. She remembered the dream, night after night, turned to full-fledged nightmare. Herself alone, on foot. Flame and smoke wherever she turned. No cat, no raven overhead. No figure on a gray horse. Herself then, struggling along a path, overgrown with brambles that snagged her sweater, dragged at her legs and arms. Last night the path had dwindled into darkness, so deep that at last she had had to stop and drag herself out of dream, out of sleep. She had lain awake in the quiet darkness of her room, lost. Alone again. Alone.

LAUREL MOUNTAIN CENTER FOR RESEARCH AND REHABILITATION

August 16, 2000
Noah and Abigail Periodes
Global Family Group Home
Laurel Mountain Center

Dear Drs. Periodes,

It is with deep personal regret that I request your resignations, effective immediately. As you know, I had great hopes for the GFGHP. Now, however, of the four children chosen for the project and placed in your sole care, one is gravely ill and another missing and, according to the state police, presumed dead. Furthermore, I have listened to the tapes of your official family meetings, and though Dr. Turnbull did his best to represent this "work" as possibly paradigm-shifting research, I can only consider it psychological malpractice. You encouraged and even fed in these four children the very fantasies and delusions it was your absolute responsibility to dispel. I have requested the destruction of all copies of these tapes and the sealing of all GFGHP records, electronic or hard copy, as a direct threat to the scientific reputation of this facility. I remind you that those records belong to Laurel Mountain and not to you.

Since the Global Family Group Home is your primary residence, you may have two weeks to find another place to live. You will not, during this time, be permitted to see patients.

Your discretion in this matter will avoid unpleasantness both for Laurel Mountain and for yourselves.

Sincerely,

Harold Deitz, President of the Board and Foundation Chair
cc: Harlan Turnbull, M.D., Ph.D.

P.O. BOX 1295 LAUREL RIDGE, NEW YORK 12929 (518) 555-4500

*I've been sitting since midnight, staring out into the darkness,
watching the moon path on the lake, listening to the wind in
the trees, like the sound of a waterfall. I can't look anymore,
knowing this is the last time. I heard a loon cry a little while
ago, the loneliest sound in the world. It hurt my bones to
hear it.*

*Armageddon. Yes. This must be what it feels like to be
caught in a war. Everything's being destroyed, and there's
nothing I can do about it. Though it didn't get much play
against the highway bombings, the search for Elijah did get on
the national news, and Mother and Daddy are not only afraid
Laurel Mountain's surrounded by anarchist crazies, they're
furious with Turnbull and the Periodeses and anybody else they
can think of to blame. Daddy's using words like* NEGLIGENCE
and MALPRACTICE *and threatening lawsuits. They're coming
tomorrow (today now) to take me—"home," they call it. I don't
have a home anymore.*

This was home. This was family.

*It's like being torn apart. Dismembered. Like a grenade
went off in the middle of the Ark, and we've all been blown to
bits. I think maybe I'm bleeding to death.*

*Doug's leaving, too. Devereux's his primary now, and
Doug's work in the computer lab has convinced him that he's
ready to go. He's going to stay with his old math teacher and
see Devereux twice a week as an outpatient.*

Noah and Abigail don't know yet where they'll go. They

look shell-shocked, both of them. The only way Doug and I can even stay in this house till we leave is if Noah and Abigail don't talk about anything important—connections, family.

I can't even think about Taryn and Elijah. It hurts too much.

Moft.

> *!talkD: Moft.*

You okay?

> *No.*

Sorry, stupid question. You still having the dream?

> *Nightmare. That's why I'm still awake. I don't want to take any chances.*

I just woke up from it. No horse, no ax. I don't even have the whistle anymore. Are we ever going to sleep again?

> *Maybe not.*

So much for the quest.

> *No! I've been thinking and thinking about that. Awful as it is, we're still dreaming. If the quest had been blown up with everything else, wouldn't the dream be gone, too?*

?

> *Do you know the story of the Holy Grail?*

Vaguely.

> *The knights couldn't start the quest for the Grail together. Each one had to start alone. In the darkest part of the woods. Maybe that's what's happening to us.*

The darkest part of the woods. It sure feels like it.

> *Yes.*

So then what? What are we supposed to do?

I don't know. Survive. Go to screen-saver mode.
Chaos patterns.
If this isn't chaos, I don't know what is.
Miranda—
?
I'll miss you.
!!!!!! All the languages I know and I don't have words for this.
Maybe there aren't any.
Mother and Daddy get here early tomorrow—this morning. There won't be any time to be alone.
It's better that way.
I have to stop now. I'm crying on my keyboard. Doug, what are we going to do?
What you said. Survive.
I guess.
:-o
What's that?
A kiss. :-o
:-o
Ktum, Miranda.
Ktum.

Quest

Journal—Miranda Ellenby
October 1, 2008

The raven.

It was the raven that began it all over again—in a dream that was the past reaching out and grabbing me. Waking me up in a cold sweat, my heart pounding in my throat. Waking me up.

And suddenly, as if I had no say in the matter at all, I found myself taking that job Henri's been offering me since I finished the doctorate and agreed to grow up. How to explain it? A raven flies into my dreams and I give up good money, a perfectly wonderful Paris apartment in a high-security building, a comfortable corporate job, and come back to the States, something I swore I would never, never do.

October first. I'm starting a journal again, in English this time, with nobody left to hide from. Would I even remember enough Muktuluk to do it the old way?

Here I sit in a tiny apartment in the middle of central Manhattan, a besieged city inside a city, fenced off from the dangers outside and protected by the largest urban police force in the world. Miranda K. Ellenby, ex-phenom, working for a UN agency so tiny the secretary general barely remembers its existence. Crazy!

No, no. Not crazy. Not me! I have proof. An official life history, thanks to Mother and Daddy's fame and money, with no trace of the months at Laurel Mountain. A summer of my life wiped out with the touch of a delete key.

It was a summer I deleted, too, working so hard to forget that when I woke from watching the raven circle down out of a darkening sky, I had to struggle to put a name to the image, a person to the name. Elijah Raymond. Eight years old, and gone eight years ago.

Bits of that summer are coming back—so clear but so distant they could be scenes from a book I read in another lifetime, except for the pain that lurks around all the edges. Except for the loss. Like losing my arms and legs. A loss so intense I had to cauterize the stumps to keep from bleeding to death.

A lake. A mountain with its cap of clouds, pink with sunrise. The call of loons and the rush of wind in the firs. A smell I have never found in all the world again, of cedar and hemlock, pine and balsam and damp moss. And the odd, hollow booming of the Adirondack ground underfoot.

Abigail. A needlepoint cheetah running forever across a grassy plain. The real cheetahs are gone now, with only images like that needlepoint left to remind us. A cat that could run 70 mph—like the unicorn, an image too strange to have ever been real. Did she ever finish it?

Last I heard, Noah and Abigail were in California, building a private practice out there, where nothing was too strange to be believed by someone. I don't even know if they survived the quake. Could be they, too, like wild cheetahs, like Mother and Daddy, are extinct.

Taryn. Did she get away? Did the drugs turn off her ears forever, so she'd never hear the stars again? Did they scramble the brain that made the poetry, turn off the energy that held us together? She would be eighteen now. Too old for Laurel Mountain.

Harlan Turnbull, M.D., Ph.D. What did we call him? The Grape. Daddy sent me a clipping years ago. Sanctioned for using unapproved drugs and fired—Harold Deitz's last act before resigning. Poor Grape. He never even came near a Nobel Prize!

And Doug. Wolves survive.

Like a knight setting out into the deepest part of the forest alone, I've been in darkness. In that darkness I put myself to sleep. But now I am awake.

October 3, 2008 _____

MIRANDA CLIMBED THE STAIRWAY, crushed between the others hurrying upward from the trains, as if they were late for something important, plotting to be the first through security, first to the taxi stand, first out the doors to the street. She was in no hurry, carried along in the rush. Her business for the day, such as it was, was over, and there was nothing to do now but get back to her apartment, check the messages on her vid screen, fix something to eat, and record another day of frustration in her journal. Corporate life had been easy compared to this.

Ahead of her, through the scanners, the crowd expanded outward into the vast open space of Grand Central Station. She was able to take a breath and slow her pace. She had missed lunch. There was nowhere in the station to get the baguettes she had come to love in Paris, but there was a bagel shop. A bagel and a cup of decaf would do, she thought.

She angled to her left, away from the sweep of the steps that led to Vanderbilt Avenue, and crossed the vast open space, wind-

227

ing her way through the streams of people moving in every direction. Suddenly she stopped, so abruptly that a man crashed into her back and cursed as he zigzagged around her. Above the noise of the crowd and the unintelligible drone of a track-change announcement floated the faint silvery tones of a flute. She strained to see through the moving bodies to the source of the sound but could not.

Forgetting bagel and coffee, she moved toward the sound. The image of a wooden whistle formed in her mind, a whistle twined with carvings of leaves and flowers. As the sound became clearer, memory and something else—a sense of certainty—drew her forward. The player was improvising, a liquid sound that felt familiar, as if the images it wove were images of her own past, and her heart began to beat against her ribs.

Doug, she thought as she saw ahead a cluster of people standing in a semicircle around a musician against the wall near the passage that led to the subway tracks. *Doug.* Holding her breath, she pushed her way into the crowd.

When she had jostled herself to the front, ignoring the elbows that jostled back, she sagged like a deflated balloon. The musician was a pale-faced girl, dressed all in black, her long blond hair flowing over her shoulders. On the floor in front of her lay a flute case, a few bills and coins scattered across its velvet interior.

What was I thinking of? she asked herself disgustedly. Had she really thought that the sound had meant Doug McAllister, as if he was the only person in America to play the flute? The raven dream had rattled her senses.

Miranda dug into her pocket for a dollar to drop into the case. Then she moved quickly out of the crowd. But she did not leave.

The music held her, sending tendrils of memory to bind her to this stranger. She slipped her leather shoulder bag between her body and the wall for safekeeping and leaned against the marble, closing her eyes to let the music's images come.

She saw long, rolling hills and grasses, a river—and then, quite suddenly, an image of the musician herself, but from another perspective. She could see part of the girl's back, the hair like a golden curtain against the black sweater, the slim fingers moving against the flute, and the girl's left cheek. Miranda felt her own fingers twitch, moving as if she were playing the air as the girl played, as if her fingers knew the feel of the keys, and then—suddenly—curling into fists. Miranda opened her eyes and blinked. Still the image of the girl was in her mind. She looked and saw the girl herself, superimposed on the image, as if she were looking at her from the left and right at once. Behind the alternate image, like looking into a distant mirror, she saw herself leaning against the wall. And felt a wave of dizziness.

She blinked and blinked again to chase away the phantom image, to look at the girl not with her mind but with her eyes. Only with her eyes. And saw him, standing a little way from the crowd, his whole body tense with listening. A young man, tall and broad-shouldered, in jeans and a windbreaker, running shoes, a leather pack hanging from one shoulder. Long black hair pulled back, both hands clenched in fists as she herself had felt them clench a moment ago.

He looked up and their eyes met. Locked. The eyes, even from this distance, of a trapped wolf. Miranda was glad of the wall she leaned against. Time seemed to stop, except that the sound of the flute went on, wrapping itself around them.

When the song was over a smattering of applause, a few more bills dropped into the flute case, and the listening crowd began to move away. Miranda stayed where she was and let him come to her.

"Miranda Ellenby," he said, his voice the same, but deeper. "Baby Genius."

"*Dr.* Ellenby," she said, forcing the words past a constriction in her throat.

He put out his hand, the white scar a jagged line across the wrist beneath his jacket cuff. "Dr. McAllister here," he said, as his hand closed around hers. *"Moft."*

"Moft."

October 3, 2008 _____

THE WAITER SET DOWN MIRANDA'S bagel and Doug's scone. "Anything else? Sweetener for your coffee?" They shook their heads and he hurried away.

At first, as they climbed past the guards, out of the station, and into the damp, acrid air outside, they had said little, too stunned at finding each other to get further than an agreement to find a coffee shop. Then Miranda had told of her raven dream, and they had not stopped talking since.

"It was math, computers, and music," Miranda said now, and sipped her coffee. "How could you let the music go?"

"The same way you could go to Paris and make yourself forget. Screen-saver mode, remember? Besides, I didn't have a choice. I found I couldn't play. The music wouldn't come. I tried to play other people's music, but the sound of the flute—at least when I played it—was like nails on a blackboard. All jagged edges."

"So math won. Clean and pretty—"

"And reliable. I teach it that way now, at the Institute for Higher Mathematics. Nothing so messy as feelings. Nothing so dangerous as human motives. It's a faculty full of baby geniuses, by the way. At twenty-five, I'm practically an old man. And you should see the students! The youngest is nine." Doug broke open his scone and spread it with butter. "Pretty threatening for a Phenom of the Century."

Miranda smiled. "It was a different century."

"So it was. Why the UN?"

"My mentor at the Sorbonne is involved with the agency."

"So what does it do, this agency?"

Miranda sighed. "You should ask what it tries to do. There's no money. It works for children, and no one thinks children are worth making a priority. Children don't vote. They don't control money. They don't command armies and weapons. And no matter how many the world loses, there are always more of them. So most of what we do is try to find people who can do what children need to have done and then persuade them to do it for free. Doctors, teachers, counselors, caregivers. Half the time they not only have to work without pay, but scrounge the materials and supplies they need to do the work."

"What do *you* do?"

Miranda laughed. "What do you think? I talk. In whatever language they need. When I finish the training they can theoretically send me anywhere in the world to try to turn 'skilled and capable professionals' into volunteer humanitarians. Today was

231

my second solo run. I spent three hours with an Armenian doctor who's visiting relatives in Connecticut, trying to persuade him to spend a month in a refugee camp, fighting typhoid."

"And?"

"Let's just say he isn't yet convinced." Miranda bit into her bagel and looked out into the gray light of the narrow street, where yellow taxis jockeyed for position. A bicycle messenger threaded his way between the cars, slipping through spaces that seemed impossibly narrow. "That's the agency," she said, "always looking for the cracks."

They ate and drank their coffee without speaking then, avoiding each other's eyes, until the bagel and the scone were gone and the waiter had refilled their mugs. Doug spoke at last. "For a while I tried to hold on to what you'd said about the quest, about needing to start alone. But it didn't work. If we're alone there *isn't* a quest."

"We aren't alone now."

Doug nodded. "So what does it mean, finding each other like this?"

"Could be just coincidence. We both had perfectly good reasons for being there," Miranda said.

"And perfectly good reasons to stop and listen to a flute player. You know what I mean. I dreamed the raven, too."

"So it's happening again." Miranda blew on her steaming coffee. "I had a sense of you—I even thought when I got through the crowd to see who was playing the flute it might be you. And then I beat myself up for thinking anything so stupid."

Doug nodded. "I began thinking of you the night of the dream. And today, all day, I felt a kind of pressure to do something, except that I didn't know what. The truth is, I left early—canceled my office hours because I couldn't concentrate anymore. I shouldn't have been coming through the station for another hour and a half."

"So what do we do now?"

Doug shrugged. "I'm not sure we have a lot of choice here. Do you remember that image Taryn had, of the magnet? We're being drawn back. Whatever is happening, it's happening."

"So we just do what we have to do, the way I had to take this job."

"Right. And keep in touch." He reached across the table and took her hand. An image moved between them—the peeling swimming raft, rocking on the water beneath the mountain. They both smiled. "We've grown up. It's our choice now."

Miranda dug into her bag and produced a card. "So you'll know how to reach me."

"You don't trust coincidence and dreams?"

"Or magnets. Have you tried anything—anything like what we were doing at the Ark—with your students? Or the baby geniuses on the institute's faculty? Thinking together? Sharing images? Reaching?"

"These are mathematicians," Doug said. "Hardheaded, rational, linear—"

"Have you?"

He sighed and shook his head. "Screen-saver mode. I turned it off the way I put away my flute."

"And now it's turned itself back on. Maybe you should start asking them some questions."

Doug finished his coffee. "Maybe."

"Eight years," Miranda said.

"Eight years." He picked up the bill. "You want to walk awhile?"

Miranda smiled. "Yeah, let's."

October 9, 2008 _____

SUBJECT: Weekend Plans?
FROM: "DOUGLAS McALLISTER" <dmcall@highl.instmth.edu>
DATE: Thurs, 9 Oct 2008 19:39:19 -0400 (EDT)
TO: Miranda Ellenby

Anything on for this weekend? I've got a car (on loan from one of the baby geniuses). We could go up to the mountains. D.

SUBJECT: Re Weekend Plans?
FROM: "MIRANDA ELLENBY" <Mirellen@childwel.UNchil.org>
DATE: Thurs, 9 Oct 2008 19:54:12 -0400 (EDT)
TO: Doug McAllister
Not Laurel Mountain! And anyway, is it safe? M.

SUBJECT: Re Weekend Plans?
FROM: "DOUGLAS McALLISTER" <dmcall@highl.instmth.edu>
DATE: Thurs, 9 Oct 2008 20:42:11 -0400 (EDT)
TO: Miranda Ellenby

Of course not Laurel Mountain! Nothing's safe. D.

234

SUBJECT: *Re Weekend Plans?*
FROM: *"MIRANDA ELLENBY" <Mirellen@childwel.UNchil.org>*
DATE: *Thurs, 9 Oct 2008 20:44:15 -0400 (EDT)*
TO: *Doug McAllister*

Okay. M.

October 10, 2008 _____

As Miranda listened to the rush of Armenian from the other end of the phone she kept the image in her mind, focusing as much of her attention as she could spare from the task of under-standing the man's argument. A little girl in a torn and ragged nightgown, dark eyes enormous in a malnourished face, dark hair curling down over her forehead. The child sat in the corner of a dirty crib, holding her arms up as if begging to be lifted, to be hugged and comforted. Tears streaked her narrow face. The message radiated from the image—*alone and sick and desperate,* it said, *alone!*

The idea had come to her that morning in the shower. She had asked Doug if he had tried it—reaching—images flowing between minds. Why not try herself? This man was a hotshot doctor with a hotshot mind. Maybe he had never been a baby genius, but she didn't know that. And she didn't know if it even mattered. It was worth a try, she had thought, turning off the water. Definitely worth a try.

When the man wound down—and that was exactly what it

235

sounded like to her, as if, moment by moment, he was losing energy—she repeated an argument she had made to him the day before. And let the child in her mind struggle to pull herself up, holding to the bars of the crib. Standing, balanced precariously, the child reached up with both emaciated arms.

And then the man asked a question. And another. How many children were in the camp? How many infants? What drugs were available?

Miranda kept the image in place until she'd hung up the phone, then relaxed, sinking into her chair with a sigh. After a moment, she jabbed the air with her fist. "Yes!" she said to her startled boss, who was working at a screen across the tiny office. "He's not only going to do it, his brother's hospital is going to donate all the drugs he needs!"

October 11, 2008 _____

DOUG HAD TURNED THE JEEP off the Northway, and they were winding into the Adirondacks on a two-lane state road in a steady stream of traffic. "I'd forgotten the leaf-peepers," Doug said, talking over the wind and the sound of the engine. "Half the world comes to the mountains every fall to see the colors. Militia or no militia." The day was so warm and golden they had driven all the way from the city with the windows open.

"Where are we headed?" Miranda asked now, scanning the map she had open in her lap. "Same place everybody else is going?"

"I hope not. There's a trail I like—up Moose Mountain—just

236

past Saranac Lake. The trailhead's hard to find, so we should have it to ourselves."

Miranda found the place on the map. "I see Moose Mountain. Three thousand nine hundred and twenty-one feet, it says." She looked down at the boots she had bought for this trip. "We don't have to go all the way to the top, do we?"

"We don't have to do anything we don't want to."

"I know one thing I do want to do—stop for lunch. Soon."

"In that case, it'll have to be Lake Placid." Doug stepped on the brake as the cars in front of him slowed. "At this rate we'll be lucky to make it that far before we starve."

Half an hour later, as traffic crept through Lake Placid, Doug turned in front of a New Jersey tourist signaling to cross the stream of traffic and took the parking spot that had just opened up in the municipal lot. "That's what he gets for being on the wrong side of the street!" he said as he pocketed the ignition key. "Now if we can just find a table in a restaurant."

"It's like midtown Manhattan before they banned private cars," Miranda said as they wound their way through the crowds on the sidewalk. "I didn't know towns up here had big-city problems."

"They do when all the city people are here! When I was a kid *big city* up here meant Montreal. That was before the militia got so big, of course."

Miranda nodded. Twice in the last two hours they had passed military convoys heading north to the border-patrol outposts.

They found a restaurant with no line on the sidewalk outside, and only a fifteen-minute wait inside. "Another minute and I'd have been a goner," Miranda whispered when they were finally shown to a table by the windows overlooking the street. She picked up the menu. "Vegetarian! No wonder the line was so small. Are you still a vegetarian?"

Doug looked at her over the top of the menu. "After Taryn—are you kidding? Of course I'm a vegetarian!"

"I got away from it myself. It comes from living in Paris. Coquilles St. Jacques, escargots, boeuf bourguignon."

"Take my advice, then—skip the soy burger."

Having talked on the road since seven in the morning, they ate without speaking, watching the tourists go by on the street. "Funny, isn't it?" Miranda said when she'd finished her beans and rice and was sipping the tea she'd ordered instead of dessert.

"What?"

"I spent only a few months of my life in these mountains. But this feels like coming home. There have been lots of people in my life in the last eight years, but they haven't really been there. I haven't let them in."

Doug nodded. "A professor once called me a pathological introvert. He said I never interacted with people at all, I just inhabited the same spaces sometimes. He was right. I don't even interact much with the little geniuses at the institute. I just haven't wanted—" He stopped speaking and pushed a parsley sprig around on his plate with his fork.

"Connections?" Miranda finished for him. He nodded. "If you connect with people you risk having the connections broken," she said, and breathed in the cinnamon scent of her tea. "The same for me. But here we are."

The waiter brought the check. "My turn," Miranda said, handing over her card. She pointed out the window. "You want to check out that shop across the street?" she asked. "It's called The Ark!"

Doug nodded. "I noticed."

When they'd made their way through the two almost-stationary lines of traffic outside, they stood in front of the store's window a moment. In the center was a huge wooden ark, a traditional design. Individually carved wooden figures of animals filled the decks and the windows of the ark's cabin.

Around it were posters, stuffed animals, sculptures, framed watercolors, note cards, books, and calendars, all depicting animals extinct in the wild. A sign proclaimed that twenty percent of the proceeds from sales went to the World Wildlife Fund. Miranda looked at a poster of a mother elephant, her trunk wrapped around her baby's body, as if to protect it from the camera. "They went so fast," she said, "all the big animals. It's hard to believe there aren't any more except in zoos and a couple of game parks."

"A pretty pitiful way to try to save the world. That's the problem with the Ark story in the first place, you know—two of every species isn't enough. The gene pool's way too small."

Miranda sighed. "You want to go inside?"

"How could we not?"

As she pushed open the door a delicate chiming sound and the scent of spicy incense greeted them. On the wall facing them was a huge banner, its message constructed of pairs of animals twined together to form the letters. WELCOME TO THE ARK, it said. The W that began the message was a pair of human beings; they were sitting on the ground, facing each other, with their knees up.

"Humans," Doug said. "Just another species that needs saving."

"And there's no Captain Noah to sail the ark," Miranda said. She looked from the banner to the ink-and-watercolor drawings scattered among the posters on the walls. "The same artist," she said.

A man with a sandy beard and mustache stood by the cash register, keeping an eye on the customers who were browsing among the display tables. "The artist is here now," he said to Miranda, "if you'd like to meet her." He pointed toward an alcove at the back of the shop, where a woman sat working at an easel, her back to them.

Miranda started forward and then stopped. The woman was very slim, not tall, dressed in jeans and a batik top, her black hair pulled together at the base of her neck with a heavy barrette. A thin café au lait–colored left hand held the brush, moving it with sure, swift strokes. Miranda reached for Doug's hand just as he was reaching for hers.

"It isn't!" Miranda whispered.

The figure turned around then, green eyes vibrant and unmistakable in a young woman's face. "Taryn!" Doug and Miranda said together.

She smiled. "Welcome to the Ark. I wondered when you'd come."

October 11, 2008 _____

WHEN DOUG AND MIRANDA HAD recovered from the shock, taken turns hugging and being hugged, they invited Taryn to hike with them. She took a few minutes to put away her paints, collected a sweater, and waved to the man behind the counter as they passed him. "These are the friends I told you about." As she climbed into the backseat of the Jeep, she said, "Jerry and Marge will do dinner. I live in what used to be their barn—you're welcome to spend the night."

"You were expecting us," Doug said as he squeezed the Jeep into the stream of cars. His eyes met Taryn's in the rearview mirror, and he blinked. He had forgotten the intensity of those eyes. Taryn nodded and settled back into the seat. "I didn't know when you'd come, only that you would."

"Of course you did," he muttered.

While they made their way through the stop-and-start traffic of Lake Placid and out onto the highway, Taryn answered Miranda's and Doug's questions. No, Turnbull hadn't kept her drugged for long (a few months, she thought, though she couldn't be sure of time), and no, the drugs hadn't done any permanent damage. "Things were fuzzy for a while afterward, but finally they cleared."

Threatening to use drugs again if she didn't cooperate, Turnbull had tried to study her powers. "He kept it all a secret, of course. He couldn't let anyone know he took it seriously. When I got the idea that he wanted to 'sell' me to the CIA as some sort of secret weapon I stopped the whole thing."

Miranda was turned in her seat, keeping her eyes on Taryn, as if she were a fantasy that would vanish if she looked away for a moment. "How did you stop it?"

Taryn grinned. "I scared him. It's easy to scare somebody who's willing to destroy other people, because he believes everyone else is willing to destroy him."

Doug laughed. "And he thought you could really do that!"

Taryn's eyes met his in the mirror again. She didn't laugh with him. "I could have. He knew it. What he didn't know was that I wouldn't." After a moment, she grinned again. "Besides, he was doing a perfectly good job of destroying himself. It just took a few years longer."

Devereux had become her primary when Turnbull left. It was Devereux who arranged to have a painter come to give her art lessons, found a publisher for her poetry, and introduced her to Jerry and Marge so that when she was old enough to leave Laurel Mountain she would have a place to go. "He never knew what we called the group home," she said. "That Jerry and Marge's shop is named The Ark is pure coincidence."

Doug snorted. "Yeah, the way apples just happen to fall down instead of up when they drop off the tree."

"I'll never think of anything as 'coincidence' again," Miranda said. "Did you stay in touch with the kids on the networks?"

"I never touched a computer again at Laurel Mountain. But the connections are building again now. I'm back in touch with Jacob and Violeta and Akeylah."

"Computer connections?" Doug asked.

"That's how it started. Jacob's brother runs a network we've been using as home base. Last month Siobhan and Liam turned up. They're at university now, and they have twin cousins, just seven years old, that they wanted to connect with me. We used computers the first time, and after that—" Taryn stopped, looking up at the orange-and-gold stretch of mountainside out her car window.

"After that?" Miranda prompted.

242

"You could say that Tim and Moira learn faster than we did. And they don't like having to turn their ideas and images into words for a computer. So they don't bother with it."

Doug pulled off the highway into an unmarked gravel turnout where another car was parked. "Looks like we won't have the trail to ourselves after all," he said.

Taryn turned to look at the car. After a moment, she gathered up her sweater, opened the door, and got out, shaking her head. Her dark hair gleamed in the sunlight. "They're fishing," she said, "not hiking."

Doug pulled his and Miranda's jackets out from behind his seat and locked the car doors. "You *sense* this?" he asked.

Taryn laughed and pointed to a clutter of fishing paraphernalia in the back of the car. "Plain old logical deduction," she said. "Let's go climb a mountain."

October 11, 2008 _____

TARYN SAT IN THE SUN, her arms wrapped around her knees, staring out across the autumn-colored valley to the blue-gray of the distant peaks. Her sweater sleeves tied around her waist, she had climbed as nimbly as a goat, seemingly without effort, and had reached this vantage point, a shelf of rock above a sheer cliff, long before the other two. Miranda, still gasping for breath from the last and steepest part of the climb, sank down beside her and brushed her damp hair back from her forehead. Doug pulled a water bottle from his pack and handed it to Miranda before perching on a nearby boulder.

Miranda took a drink and handed the bottle to Taryn. She leaned back on her hands and looked at the panorama spread beneath and in front of them. "Incredible. What a glorious day!"

"There won't be many more like it," Doug said. "It's almost winter on the high peaks."

"It wouldn't be comfortable on the top even now," Taryn said. "Not with just sweaters and jackets. It's probably twenty degrees colder up there."

Miranda looked across the valley, with its greens and golds, oranges and reds. Sun glinted off the curves of a river that wound through fields of golden grasses close beneath them. "Who needs to go farther up?"

For a long time the three of them sat, quiet, looking across to the mountains, rank on rank, fading into the blue distance, stilled by the beauty stretched before them.

"It's as if I'm breathing this," Miranda said at last. "As if I need it to live."

"Look at the leaves!" Taryn said. "I've never seen that before."

It took the others a moment to see what she was talking about. And then they saw. Leaves of brilliant gold, caught in eddies of wind above the trees, were rising steadily up the cliff face, spiraling upward into the sky.

"Like butterflies," Miranda said. "Like golden birds."

Taryn grinned up at Doug. "Falling *up*," she said.

"Okay, okay," he said. "But they aren't apples!"

Miranda took another sip of water and handed the bottle back to Doug. "Did you dream the raven, too?" she asked Taryn.

Taryn nodded. "A couple of weeks before I left Laurel Mountain. Several more times since."

"They never found him, did they? Elijah."

"They never found him."

"He's gone." Doug drank from the bottle, offered it to the others, and capped it when they declined. He put it into his pack. "How could he have survived out there by himself? He was so little."

"He isn't gone," Taryn said. "The raven's flying."

Miranda dragged her eyes from the spiraling golden leaves and looked at Taryn. "Do you mean that symbolically? That the quest lives on? Or do you mean Elijah's actually alive out there somewhere?"

"Of course he's alive. Don't you feel him?" Taryn tightened her grip on her knees and put her head down for a moment, her body still, as if she was listening to something. The image of the raven, its wings beating slowly against a vast sky, filled their minds. When Taryn looked up, her eyes were sparkling in their green intensity. "You see? He's flying. I didn't know until I had the dream. But now I can feel it. All the time."

"But where is he?" Doug said. "The three of us are together again. And he's not here."

"That doesn't mean he's dead."

"That's wishful thinking," Doug said, his voice tight. "A dream! He couldn't have survived in the mountains alone." He pushed himself to his feet and walked to the edge of the rock ledge, staring down over the cliff, where the leaves still swept upward like bits of ash above a campfire. He kicked at a patch of lichen on the rock. "I can't feel him."

"He hasn't found us yet," Taryn said. "Yesterday you hadn't found me, but I felt you. Knew you were coming."

A wind swept up the cliff face and blew around them, scattering leaves, chilling them despite the sun. A deep, hollow sound began, as if the wind was whistling among the outcroppings of rock. The sound grew until for each of them the valley, the distant mountain peaks and ridges, blanked out suddenly. Darkness surrounded them.

Then there was no more mountain, no warm autumn sun. They saw a sea of faces, contorted by rage. Faces with murderous eyes. Dark gray clouds loomed overhead, and a fine spray of rain struck them with cold. Buildings lined both sides of a narrow cobblestone street. A mob of raging people armed with sticks, brooms, rakes, and shovels surged toward them, bloodthirsty eyes focused on something over their shoulders, something behind them. Eerily, the mob came in silence, the only sound the wailing of the wind in a mountain no longer beneath their feet.

"The lion!" It was Taryn's voice, coming to Doug and Miranda as if from a great distance through the wailing of the wind. "See the lion!"

As her words were whipped away on the rising wind, the mob dissolved before them and the image of the lion appeared, its massive head filling their field of vision. It charged, a bounding golden mass of power, with gleaming teeth and paws as big as their heads, claws extended as it leapt. The huge cat crashed into them, claws tearing their chests. Pain threatened to send them reeling backward, alone into darkness.

With an effort of will they flung their arms around the lion's neck, pressing their faces into the thick fur, forcing the heavy body back. They pushed their hands into the coarse mane. *Down,* they said, struggling to keep their voices calm, *down, boy. Easy. Take it easy.*

246

Jaws gaped above their heads, and they braced against the thought of teeth, braced against losing, against dying. But the weight shifted, the huge paws dropped to the ground, and the lion sank to its haunches. Golden eyes blinked up at them. The wind dropped into silence. Darkness closed in.

Miranda opened her eyes. Doug was sprawled on the rock near the edge of the cliff, his eyes screwed shut. After a moment, he blinked and looked over at her. They turned to Taryn, whose eyes were wide and blank.

Doug tried to push himself up, but his arms had no strength. He dragged himself away from the edge of the cliff and lay on his stomach, breathing hard. Miranda, who had been sitting cross-legged, stretched out her legs and lowered herself slowly to the rock so that she was lying on her back, her arm over her eyes to shield them from the sun. Taryn did not move.

The air grew colder as the sun moved down the sky, casting dark shadows across the valley, and still they did not move.

At last Taryn shook herself, blinked a few times, and brushed her bangs from her forehead with a shaking hand. "Tim and Moira," she said. "We were seeing that mob through their eyes."

Miranda moved her arm and turned stiffly toward Taryn, her neck and shoulders as taut and sore as if she'd been lifting weights. "What was it all about? Who were they after? And what happened?"

Taryn spread her hands helplessly. "I don't know."

Doug struggled to a sitting position and rolled his head on his neck to work out the stiffness. "The seven-year-old twins? You've told them about taming the lion?"

Taryn shook her head. "I've hardly talked to them at all. But it wasn't only them. All of us—Jacob and Violeta and Akeylah. Siobhan and Liam. A couple of others, too, that I don't know. And Elijah. From the first moment, Elijah. I don't mean any of them were *there*. Not literally there on the street where the twins were. Wherever they really were, wherever their bodies were, they got pulled in just the way we did."

"What about the lion?"

Taryn rubbed at her face with both hands. "They heard me somehow. When we saw the lion, we made it strong enough for them to see it, too. Then they just did what we did, as if we were teaching them, showing them how."

"I want to know if it worked," Miranda said.

"I think we'd know if it didn't." Taryn smiled a tiny, tired smile that grew until it lighted her whole face. "We'd know if it didn't!" She looked from Miranda to Doug and back, her face radiant in the orange glow of the sinking sun. "We've finally begun!" she said.

October 13, 2008 _____

SUBJECT: Quest
FROM: "DOUGLAS McALLISTER" <dmcall@highl.instmth.edu>
DATE: Mon, 13 Oct 2008 8:15:27 -0400 (EDT)
TO: Miranda Ellenby

Just pulled this off the nets—thought you and Taryn would want to see it. She's right. It's started. D.

Path:

instmth.edu.com!netnews.harvard.edu!birddog.srv.cs.smu.edu!ABERDEEN
.AC.UK! bass!internews

From: internews@globenet.com (AP)

Distribution: inter.apo

Message-ID: <Belfast-mobUR482_431@globenet.com>

Date: Sat, 11 Oct 08 8:30GMT

> BELFAST (AP)—What may be the oddest occurrence in the long
> and bloody history of "the troubles," as they're called
> here, happened on the streets of Belfast early this evening.
> Two young IRA members, convicted of a pub bombing that broke
> the most recent cease-fire and claimed eleven lives, were
> being transported to prison when the prison van broke down
> on a street edging an often-volatile Protestant
> neighborhood.
>   Passersby assaulted the guards and dragged the prisoners,
> shackled hand and foot, into the street. In a matter of moments
> an angry mob had gathered, clamoring for blood. As the mob closed
> in, witnesses say, it was clear the prisoners would not escape
> with their lives.
>   But suddenly, without any apparent explanation, the advancing
> mob stopped, milled around in confusion, and then melted away,
> disappearing down streets and alleys. By the time police arrived
> the astonished guards and prisoners were standing in an empty
> street.
>   A guard who was injured in the incident said the situation
> changed suddenly when two small children, a boy and a girl,

249

> emerged from a nearby house and stood by the shackled men. "They
> did nothing nor said nothing, just stood there, looking. I told
> them to get on out before they were hurt, but they didn't go.
> Next thing, people got real quiet. It was eerie, it was. Then the
> crowd just began wandering off."
>   The children have not been identified. Like the mob, they had
> vanished when the police arrived.